# YOUR PLACE OR MINE?

The rest of the afternoon passed in agony for Sonja. The joy she should have gotten from the day had been replaced by unfulfilled need, by a sexual tension that left her taut as a bowstring.

Cole suffered, too. Each time Sonja bent to stir paint or stretched to reach a spot, his desire for her mounted. He'd been focused on business for so long that he'd forgotten what lust felt like. That was the only word to describe how hot she made him.

At the end of the day the volunteer coordinator thanked everyone, passed out T-shirts to each participant, then had them board the buses for downtown.

Cole slid in next to Sonja. They sat thigh to thigh, hers bare, his jean clad. Desire hummed between them, but neither spoke a word during the fifteen minute ride. After the volunteers unloaded, Cole turned to Sonja.

"Where's your car?" he asked.

"I left it in the garage and walked over here. It's just a couple of blocks. Where's yours?"

"Right over there," he said, pointing across the street.

Cole's gaze dipped to her mouth. Then he looked into her eyes and read the answer he found there. "I live in Williamsburg. It'll take thirty-five to forty minutes to get to my house."

"I live fifteen minutes from here," she said.

Cole waited.

"You drive," she said. "I'll show you the way."

Pinnacle books by Felicia Mason

*Rhapsody*
*Seduction*
*Body and Soul*
*For the Love of You*
*Foolish Heart*

# FOOLISH HEART

# Felicia Mason

Pinnacle Books
Kensington Publishing Corp.

http://www.arabesquebooks.com

PINNACLE BOOKS are published by

Kensington Publishing Corp.
850 Third Avenue
New York, NY 10022

First Printing: December, 1998
10  9  8  7  6  5  4  3  2  1

Printed in the United States of America

*In sweet memory of my dear friends
MaryAnne Gleason and Wendy Haley.*

*And for the ones they left to cherish their memories and
remember the love: Michael, Jennifer, Ryan, and Becca;
Chris and Liz.*

# Prologue

Twenty years was a long time to wait for justice, but, finally, the day had come. Coleman Heart would be sorry he ever tangled with the Pride family.

Sonja Pride would be victorious and her struggle more than worth the wait when the entire Heart family, in particular Cole Heart, found itself bankrupt or floundering. She wanted to see them insolvent and humiliated, just the way they'd left so many others.

She'd built up her own business the old-fashioned way—with hard work and sleepless nights. Her entire career had been painstakingly calculated for this moment, the final act in a play that began long before Sonja knew words like *revenge, retribution* and *retaliate,* long before she'd tasted defeat and poverty.

"Payback is a mother," she said.

Sonja smiled and lifted a crystal champagne glass.

The light amber liquid sparkled like the determination in her eyes.

Tonight she toasted perseverance.

Soon, she'd toast sweet vengeance.

# Chapter 1

Sonja Pride's heels clicked smartly on the black marble foyer leading to the offices of Coleman Heart III. For their eight-thirty appointment, she'd arrived forty-five minutes early. She needed the extra time for the pep talk she always gave herself before meeting with a client.

And this client was special; so special that Sonja had to force herself to remember her role, to remember the cause and the plan.

She'd never met Coleman Heart III, but she had his arrogant image indelibly stamped in her memory. The research her people had done for this job was extraordinary; the results of their investigation damning. Coleman Heart's employees were robbing him blind, and he didn't even know it.

The news buoyed her already high spirits, and her smile broadened.

"Good morning."

She glanced at the man who held a glass door open for her and marked him for what he was—a Heart. He had the look—the square jaw, strong chin, and thick lashes all the males seemed to favor. This one was young, maybe in his early twenties.

She smiled at him. "Hello."

"I hope you're going my way."

"Not unless you're Coleman Heart III," she told him.

"Cole has all the luck. I'm heading to his office for a meeting, though. Follow me."

"Good morning," he called to a receptionist at the front desk.

"Good morning, Mr. Heart. Cole is waiting for you."

The younger Heart grimaced. "He's here at the crack of dawn every day. I don't think he sleeps."

"They say the early bird catches the worm," Sonja replied as she fell into step beside him.

"My uncle is here *before* the worms."

*Ah,* Sonja thought as her mental checklist clicked in. *This would be the nephew, Lance.* Brown educated, Coleman's favorite, perceived to be the heir-in-training.

Sonja glanced at the cute kid and ratcheted his age up to about twenty-five. He seemed friendly enough, was probably even a nice guy. Too bad her job was to make sure he had nothing to inherit from his long line of reprobate relatives.

She couldn't let herself get distracted about that part of the mission. Not yet.

They turned left and walked a wide, curving hallway. This was where the money lived. The carpeting was deep and luxurious. Windows outlined some of the offices in the outer circle, while an eclectic mix of art work graced the inner walls. Sonja recognized a Henry O. Tanner painting and a Varnette P. Honeywood. She spied expensive looking antiques through the open doors of one office. To the right, the wall gave way to a glass-enclosed conference room, probably where the board members met.

They passed four doors on the left before the nephew paused.

"Let me grab my pad," he said. He dashed into a smaller office and was right back with a leather portfolio.

"Right this way. My office is next to Cole's. I didn't get your name," he said.

"Sonja Pride. From The Pride Group."

The young man took her hand and pumped it. His infectious grin made Sonja smile.

"I'm Lance Heart Smith, and we've been waiting for you. Come right on in."

They passed through a small but efficient office, then into the larger one.

The first thing Sonja noticed when she stepped into Coleman Heart's private space was the absence of pretension. The simplicity hit her like a fist. After the opulence and indulgence of the inner circle and the palatial looks of some of the offices, this seemed, well, downright ordinary for a CEO. A single watercolor, a painting of either dawn or sunset, she couldn't tell which, graced the wall. A few healthy green plants were scattered about. File cabinets in a dark wood hid papers and clutter. The focal point of the room was clearly the large desk, made of cherry or some other hard wood. A PC and a smaller monitor were there, as were a telephone and neat stacks of paperwork. A comfortable looking conversation group was on one side of the room, a round conference table on the other.

This room looked as if someone actually did real work in it. While large, it was an office, not a playground for a man who kept a seat warm while collecting a paycheck and capital gains he didn't earn.

"Have a seat," Lance invited. "I'll get Cole."

Before he could turn toward the door, Cole Heart burst through it with a harried looking woman in his wake. She ripped plastic from a bag of dry cleaning as he buttoned his white shirt with one hand and yelled at someone on a cell phone in the other.

"Sell, dammit. I don't care what your recommendation is."

"Mason, get me on a plane to Aspen this weekend. I need to relax before heading to Detroit," he said.

"No, I do not want Pistons tickets," he told the person on the phone. "Just handle the stock." He snapped the phone shut and tossed it to the woman, who traded him his suit jacket for the telephone. He shrugged into the double-breasted, gray pinstripe.

"Where do you want to stay?" the woman asked.

"The usual. And make sure the car isn't a toy this time. I need space."

"I'm sorry," she said as she handed him a tie. "I thought that reservation was for—"

They both abruptly halted when they spied Lance and Sonja.

Cole looked as if he wanted to let out an expletive. The woman darted frantic eyes to her empty desk in the anteroom.

Cole took the situation under control. He strode to Sonja in bold steps and stuck out a large, strong hand.

"Good morning. You must be Sonja Pride. You're early. I like that."

Overpowering.

And god-awful sexy.

She'd seen photographs of him, usually mug shots

that accompanied newspaper stories. Nothing in her experience or expectations had prepared her for this. He stood at least six-foot-three, with broad shoulders that tapered to a narrow waist. His eyes were a dark gray. *Contacts?* she wondered. Whatever, the entire package was a presence to be reckoned with.

It took Sonja a moment to get her scattered thoughts together.

She had the advantage here, and needed to capitalize on it.

"Hello," she said.

Shaking his hand, she had to admit that everything about this man seemed larger than life. Did he eat innocent virgins for breakfast?

"Why don't you finish dressing?" She glanced at the round conference table on the other side of his desk. "I'll just set up over there. Is that all right?"

"That will be fine."

He glared at Lance, and then the hostile expression was gone. "Mason. Coffee, please."

"Yes, sir."

Moments later, fully dressed and buttoned down, Cole was at Sonja's side.

"Let's start again," he said. "I'm Cole Heart. It looks as if you've already met Lance Heart Smith." He paused with a stern look in Lance's direction, then added, "My intern."

"I'm really an executive assistant." But Lance's nervous chuckle told the story about what might be his rapidly diminishing status.

Sonja nodded. "Well, it's a pleasure to meet you both. May I plug this somewhere?" She held up a cord attached to a compact laptop.

Lance jumped to do her bidding. "Right here," he

said as he pressed a small groove in the middle of the table. An electrical socket popped up.

"Excellent."

Mason, his assistant, brought in coffee and muffins, placed them within reach on the table, then disappeared.

Cole indicated a chair for Sonja. "Well," he said, taking his own seat, "what news do you have?"

Sonja indicated the spiral-bound reports she'd placed on the table. Handing one to Cole and then one to Lance, she powered the computer. "Well, as the saying goes, I have good news and bad news."

Cole glanced at Lance, who hovered near the computer. "Is that a WinBook XLi?" the young man asked.

"Yes," Sonja said with a smile. "Top of the line. It's wonderful."

"I've been thinking about getting one of those. Is the CD-Rom drive built in?"

"Lance."

Cole's tone said, *One more distraction or screwup, and you're outta here.*

Chagrined, Lance sat and opened the report from Sonja, who indicated the laptop and nodded at him.

"Give me the bad first," Cole said.

"Well, it's not that easy," Sonja said. "Let's just start at the beginning."

Nodding his acquiescence, Cole sat back. Lance eyed the laptop.

"When you contracted with The Pride Group, you asked that we shop your stores for the total shopping experience from a customer's perspective. Over the course of two weeks, a team of eleven people worked your stores. Five shopped the three stores here in Virginia. We sent two shoppers to work the three stores in

North Carolina. Another four floated among all of the stores. We wanted to give you as broad a perspective as possible from several shopping experiences.''

"I asked that someone pose as an employee, as well,'' Cole interjected.

Sonja nodded and pressed a key to begin the Power-point presentation on the computer. "Yes, we did that too, focusing as you asked on the flagship store in Hampton and the one in the Virginia Beach area.''

"And?''

She glanced at him and decided he didn't need to be spared any details. But, oh, how she wanted to drag out the pain.

"On page three of the report, you'll see the classifications.''

Lance turned to the indicated page.

Cole simply stared at Sonja until she cleared her throat.

"Heart Federated Stores gets high marks for store design and floor layout. There's a logical, customer-oriented flow in each store.''

"Aunt Justine will be glad to hear that, huh Cole?'' Lance said. "She did all the decorating and layout,'' he added for Sonja's benefit.

A quelling look from Cole silenced Lance.

"Sorry,'' the young man murmured. He dropped his gaze back to his report.

"What's the *but*, Ms. Pride?'' Cole asked.

"The '*but*,' Mr. Heart, is that the most important asset in each of the six stores we surveyed is downplayed, sometimes outright ignored.''

"And that asset would be?''

"Your customers, Mr. Heart.''

His frown should have discouraged her, but Sonja sat

there practically giddy. Tamping down her glee and maintaining her professional decorum, Sonja continued.

"It's well documented that businesses with mediocre product but excellent customer service fare better than those with excellent product and dismal customer care. Of course, the ideal is a business atmosphere—in this case a shopping experience—that rates high marks for the quality of its products as well as its care of the customer and his satisfaction."

"How did Heart stores rate in your survey?"

"Not very well, Cole, according to this," Lance said.

Sonja's finger glided over the touchpad and two pie charts flowed onto the monitor. "On the left in green are comparable stores. On the right in blue is Heart Federated."

Cole looked at the illustration and frowned. The scowl he sent Sonja's way would have intimidated a less focused woman.

"You're telling me that customers hate everything about Heart stores?"

"Not everything. Just the way they're treated by the sales staff," she said.

"That *is* everything."

Sonja nodded. "We got the impression that there is little or no customer service or customer retention training at any of the stores."

"But what about the orientation program?" Lance asked. "That's where they're supposed to get trained. It's twenty-five hours the first week of employment, and twenty-five hours during the second week."

For once, Cole didn't scowl at Lance. He nodded in his nephew's direction then looked to Sonja for confirmation.

"The Pride Group employee assigned to the Virginia Beach store was hired there four weeks ago. Each of his scheduled training sessions has been postponed because the department manager was short-staffed on the floor. At the Hampton store, our representative was told—" Sonja consulted her notes and then read verbatim, " 'That orientation stuff isn't really important. All you need to know is how to SKU and how to run the register.' She's been there three weeks. Both employees said they did receive an hour of special training on spotting counterfeit currency. And both reported that during a lunchbreak in the employee lounge, a video on diversity awareness was playing on a continuous-loop tape. The Virginia Beach employee said the sound was muted on the VCR."

Sonja continued with her presentation, citing concrete examples and anecdotal evidence of the poor state of the Heart Department Stores. From salesclerks with attitudes to dirty rest rooms, she covered it all. By the time she finished, thunder and lightning marched across Cole's features.

"Mr. Heart, there's something else you need to know." She glanced at Lance, not sure how much to say in front of him.

"What is it?" he barked. "Lance is family."

"Employee theft is at just about thirty percent."

The explosion came, swift and sure.

"I don't know what kind of games you're playing here, Ms. Pride. I brought you in on the recommendation of a board member who thought you did good work. Don't you think I'd know if my own people were stealing from me?"

"Maybe, maybe not," she said. "I thought you might

feel this way, Mr. Heart,'' Sonja said. "I have a recommendation that I hope you'll consider."

"What?"

"When was the last time you went to a Heart store?" she asked.

Cole got up and paced the area between the table and his large desk. "I'm always in the stores. What's your point?"

Sonja sat back and crossed her legs. "Yes, you're in the stores as the chief executive officer of the company. But have you been in one as a customer lately? I suggest you go to a couple of Heart Department Stores and see for yourself."

"I'd be recognized."

"Get in disguise. It's not that difficult."

"That's ridiculous."

Sonja shut down the computer. "Mr. Heart, you hired my firm to give you a snapshot of your world. The film's been developed, and you don't like the photographs. I'm simply suggesting that you go shoot your own film, and see how your pictures fare before you discredit the very thing you requested from me. If you thought everything was rosy you never would have contacted The Pride Group."

# Chapter 2

She was right, and he knew it. That's what pissed Cole off so much. He'd already suspected every negative thing she said. Numbers didn't lie, no matter how desperately he wanted a rosier economic outlook for the company. It hurt to have an outsider waltz in and nail him in the space of a month on the very shortcomings he suspected to be the cause of depleted resources and profit from his department stores.

Cole wanted to believe it wasn't true.

He also wanted to believe that a woman as delicate as Sonja Pride would buckle when faced with his wrath. She didn't. Reluctantly, Cole admitted to himself that he liked that. A lot. Just as he admired the fact that she'd been early, even though she'd caught him not completely dressed for their appointment.

No one had caught Cole Heart unprepared for years—twenty-five to be exact—not since he was ten-years-old, and his cousin underbid him for the lease of a lemonade stand.

As Sonja sat there waiting he continued pacing the room, mulling over her recommendation and wondering why he'd noticed the way she smiled at Lance.

Suddenly, he turned to face her.

"What kind of disguise?" he asked.

"That's up to you," she said, cool as you please.

"How did your people dress?"

"It depended on their tasks. My independent shoppers went in as if they were ordinary customers. The permanent staff acted according to the guidelines you set in the initial memo you sent. Sometimes professional, sometimes scruffy, sometimes confused, at other times demanding."

"In other words, just like real customers?" Lance asked.

Sonja smiled at him. "Exactly."

Out of nowhere, a stab of jealousy attacked Cole, and the beginning of a bad mood cropped up.

"Lance, don't you have something else to do?"

"Huh?" Surprised at the tone and obviously wondering what he'd done this time, Lance looked up.

"I'd like that youth department analysis on my desk in an hour."

Lance glanced between the stony Cole and an unfazed Sonja. "Uh, okay, Cole. I'll get right on it."

He excused himself. Then, with a farewell to Sonja and one last longing look at the laptop, Lance slipped out of the office.

With the pup gone, Cole leaned two hands on the table where Sonja still sat. It was time to get to the truth.

"Why are my employees stealing from me?"

He stared at her, willing the gospel from her lips. Unflinching, Sonja met his unspoken challenge.

"Because you let them."

Cole stood up and folded his arms. Staring down his patrician nose, he studied her. Her skin was suntanned honey, a smooth light brown, darker than his own. Her wide eyes would speak volumes, given the right circumstance. He wondered what they looked like smoky with passion. Sonja Pride's full mouth begged notice. Cole decided it was best to concentrate on something else.

He would have expected her to wear red, the corporate power color. But Sonja Pride wore white. Clean, honest, virginal white. Her formfitting suit, one he recognized as *not* purchased at a Heart store, had been altered to compliment her figure.

"Where do you shop, Ms. Pride?"

Surprised, she blinked. Cole kept a small smile to himself.

"I don't see the relevance of that question," she said.

He nodded toward her suit. "That's not from a Heart Department Store."

"No, it's not," she said, meeting his challenging look.

The staring game continued. Cole conceded that he'd met a worthy adversary. His alpha responded to her omega on levels he hadn't bothered to deal with in a while. Not at all liking the flow of his thought, Cole decided to end the meeting.

"Be back here in a week," he said. "Make the appointment with Mason," he added over his shoulder as he walked to his desk chair.

Sonja stood. "Why? The Pride Group's work is complete. We've done all you requested. Extra copies of the findings are available for your board members."

She reached for the cord to unplug it from the table socket.

"*If,*" he said, stressing the word, "if your field report is accurate, your work, Ms. Pride, is just beginning."

With that he sat in his chair and punched up a program on his PC .

Sonja was dismissed.


Later, Sonja still seethed. The audacity of that arrogant son of a . . .

*Take a deep breath,* she coached herself on the drive back to her office. *You've come too far to let ego get in the way now.*

She'd taken her sweet time leaving his office. From his computer he'd scowled at her twice before she was packed up and ready to go.

When she stood in front of his desk and extended her hand to say "Good-bye", he looked as if he'd rather suck snake venom than touch her.

*So be it, you self-righteous jerk. Your day is coming, my brother. Your day is coming,* she silently fumed.

On the rest of the drive to her office, Sonja kept her mind occupied with the ways she'd celebrate Cole Heart's downfall.


The tile floors were dirty. The courtesy shopping bag racks were empty. Barely ten steps in the door, Cole counted three burned out lightbulbs in a display featuring vintage era clothing.

Making his way to the nearest cash register, he stood aside while the clerk waited on a customer.

The clerk smiled at Cole, acknowledging the new

customer's presence, then turned his attention back to his current customer.

"We don't seem to have that in stock, Ma'am. What I can do is put it on back order for you. It should take three to seven days to come in. If you'll complete this form, I'll call you when it arrives."

The customer wrote her name and number on the form then the clerk handed her a piece of paper. "I do apologize for the delay this is causing you. That's a coupon for twenty percent off any item in the store. You can use it today or save it for when the jacket comes in."

Cole watched the woman's face light up as she accepted the coupon. "Twenty percent, huh? Make my own sale. That's nice. Thank you."

"You're more than welcome."

Like an approving coach, Cole nodded. Peering through the thick glass spectacles he'd donned as part of his disguise, he made note of the employee's name: Gene. He'd done everything right. Where were Sonja Pride's people when this clerk was working? This was more like the store and the employees he knew. Sonja Pride was full of it.

As the customer moved on, Cole stepped up.

"How may I help you today, sir?" the clerk asked.

"I'm looking for a present for my, uh, wife," Cole said stroking the thick, fake mustache and beard he'd found to help shield his identity.

"Was there anything you had in mind? This is the men's department, but I can make several suggestions. Quite a few ladies like to wear mens' pajama tops."

Cole shook his head and smoothed the itchy beard. "No. I'm looking for female things. You know, something womany. Stuff that looks good and smells good."

The clerk smiled. "Let me show you how to get to our fragrance department. Right next to it you'll find women's accessories."

Gene stepped around his cash register area and walked several feet with Cole. He paused when he came to the threshold of his department. "If you stay right along this walkway you'll run into fragrances. You'll know you're in the right place when you see a display of candles. And it'll smell good."

"Well, thank you. That's mighty helpful."

"You're quite welcome. Have a pleasant Heart experience."

Cole smiled as he made his way past a display of men's hats and a bank of monitors featuring the latest mens' accessories from international designers.

Gene had provided a textbook service encounter. His customer left without what she came in the store for, but with the inconvenience coupon in hand she would probably find several things that caught her eye before she actually left the store. And she'd tell her friends about her good experience at Heart.

The clerk had just earned himself a Heart token, doled out for exemplary customer service, or doing something right. Cole remembered the first one he'd earned from his grandfather. To this day employees who earned a Heart token could redeem it for twenty-five dollars worth of store merchandise, twenty-five dollars in cash, or an hour of personal time.

Cole loved being in retail, and he loved his stores. He liked the texture of the merchandise, the colors, the music piped in on hidden speakers, the hearts embedded in the tile floors. He liked the effort put into, and the effect of, creative displays that attracted the eye. He liked making customers happy.

As he approached and paused at a clearance table of boys' shirts, Cole automatically reached out to straighten and refold the piles of merchandise. He peeked around. No one was watching, and there wasn't a clerk in sight. He made quick work of organizing the shirts. Then he meandered into the boys' department. Several customers milled about. One stood at a cash register looking around for some help. Cole recognized the signs of impatient agitation in the woman.

Where the hell were the clerks?

If he waited on the customer his cover would be blown. If he didn't, she'd leave Heart unsatisfied.

Cole figured he could mitigate the damage.

He grabbed a shirt from a rack and sidled up to her. "Hi," he said.

The woman glanced over at him. "I tell you, you can never find any help in this place," she groused.

"Ever?" Cole asked.

The woman frowned at him.

"There's a guy over there," he said, pointing to the nearby men's department. "He was real helpful. You can check out with him. Gene was his name."

"Thanks," the woman mumbled.

She scooped up about forty dollars' worth of boys' underwear and T-shirts and headed in the direction Cole had suggested.

Still no clerk. And another customer was headed to the register.

Cole bit back a frustrated curse and looked around the department. A flash of orange near the fitting room caught his eye. With the shirt in hand, he marched in that direction.

"Girl, I don't know what I'm gonna wear. When he asked me out, I was just all to pieces."

"Why don't you get something to go with that gold—"

Cole interrupted the conversation. "Excuse me, do either of you work here?"

A woman in green slacks and an orange floral top turned around. "Something I can help you with?"

He took in her name: LaKeisha. "There are people out there waiting to be waited on. And one woman just left because no one was around to help her. You need to be minding your department and customers instead of standing around gossiping."

"Excuse me." Her words weren't a polite good-bye to her co-worker.

Cole's eyes narrowed. Then he remembered his role. He held up the shirt. "Do you have this in a size eight?"

LaKeisha rolled her eyes at her friend, then went to take care of her register. The other one, Gretta, took the shirt from Cole.

"I'll check on that for you," she said.

He followed her toward the rack of Oxford cloth shirts. "How long have you worked here?" he asked.

"About a year," Gretta replied.

"What about your friend?"

The clerk searched through the shirts. "LaKeisha? She's new here. Just a couple of months." She pulled two shirts from the rack, one white and one blue.

"Would you like either of these? They're both size eight."

Cole handed her the shirt he held. "I'll take the white one."

"Anything else for you today, sir?"

"Nothing else," he said, then followed her to the two-register station.

"No, we all out of that," he heard LaKeisha say.

Cole cringed at her abuse of the language and stepped to his left so he could better watch her encounter with the customer.

"Well, is there a substitute?" the customer asked. "It's in this week's sale paper."

"We sold out. Sorry."

*Offer an alternative,* Cole screamed to himself. But LaKeisha just stood there.

Cole's scowl grew deeper. Gretta must have seen his consternation. "Is there something else I can find for you?"

"I'll look around for a minute. Your co-worker sounds like she needs some help. You seem to be out of what that lady came in for," he said.

*And your friend is going to be out of a job in the morning if she doesn't get her act together,* he added to himself.

As if she had read his thoughts, Gretta quickly moved to offer LaKeisha some help.

A few minutes later, he approached the register with the white shirt and a couple of items he'd picked up for show.

He watched as LaKeisha policed the department and Gretta waited on a customer. Gretta closed the sale the way she should have. "Thank you for your patience," she said. "Have a good rest of the day."

Cole was smiling by the time he left the boys' department. LaKeisha's longterm employment prospects were dim. As for Gretta, she hadn't earned a Heart token, but she'd redeemed herself in his eyes. The contented look left his face when he saw the messy state of the candle and stationery area and got a look at the clerk minding the area.

"What *is* this, Halloween?" he mumbled.

The woman's jet black, straight hair matched her

heavy, black, eye makeup, which matched her black lipstick, and her hideously long, black fingernails. A long black skirt and a black see-right-through-to-a-black-bra chiffon blouse completed the ghoulish and totally inappropriate get-up.

Cole's faint hope that the woman was a customer and not one of his employees flickered and died the instant she flipped her hair over her shoulder. The red and white Heart Department Store name badge was the only relief of color on the woman, and the one thing Cole didn't want to see.

He felt, actually felt, his blood pressure rising as he watched her.

Cole wanted to snatch the badge that associated her with his store. In that costume, she'd scare all the customers away.

Saying adults who worked in retail could be trusted to come to work in appropriate business attire, Cole had twice vetoed a proposal establishing a dress code for employees. Now he saw the merit in the plan. Some people had no judgment at all.

She looked as if she'd bite the head off of anyone who dared approach. Cole dared.

"Are you going to a costume party?"

The woman didn't crack a smile. "I believe in expressing the individuality of my awareness with the elements. I mourn the destruction of our planet."

"Do you work here?"

She blinked. "I am currently employed by this capitalistic stronghold."

Capitalistic stronghold? "Not for long," he snapped back. Why the hell was she working in a department store? He peered through his glasses at her name: Millicent.

"Is there an overpriced piece of shoddily-made merchandise produced by underage, underpaid, southeast Asian workers that I can find for you?" she asked.

In an instant, Cole's anger became a scalding fury. His lips thinned to a line so sharp they could cut paper.

"What the—"

A single tenuous thread of rationality and control was the only thing that kept Cole from bodily ejecting the woman from his store. How dare she stand there and spout that trash to a customer?

Without another word Cole stormed away. That Millicent creature wouldn't be on his payroll by the end of the day.

He paused near the escalators and pulled his tiny cell phone from a pocket. Mason was on the line immediately.

"I'm at the Virginia Beach store. There's a Millicent in stationery and gifts. I want her terminated by 5 P.M. Get her supervisor and his or her supervisor in my office immediately. Put all three files on my desk."

He slammed the phone shut and stared unseeing at the colorful displays near him and the people streaming by.

So furious he could hardly think straight, Cole speed-dialed his assistant again.

"Yes, sir?"

"And get Sonja Pride in my office first thing in the morning."

# Chapter 3

It took Cole a long time to calm down. The forty-minute drive to the corporate office in Hampton would have helped if he hadn't been on the telephone yelling at the Virginia Beach store manager.

Now, hours later, he still couldn't believe that a Heart employee had said the things that woman said to him. How many customers had she assaulted that way? How much damage had she done?

In the poolroom of his Williamsburg house that overlooked the gated community's world-class golf course, Cole swam laps, trying to get his still seething temper under control.

To the man's credit, the store manager had taken total responsibility. The immediate supervisor said Millicent was about to be fired, anyway. Reviewing the conversation as he swam didn't help his state of mind.

No wonder Heart stores had fared so dismally with Sonja Pride's mystery shoppers. If the company was losing money, it was because the freaking employees were sabotaging him.

Cole gave up the swimming. At this rate, he'd drown. Hauling himself from the water, he reached for a towel.

"That's some mighty aggressive swimming, cousin."

Cole had thought the day couldn't get any worse.

"Who let you in?" he asked his cousin Mallory.

"I came with your mother."

Worse took a downhill turn.

Cole's head started pounding. "What do you want?"

"Is that any way to treat family? I heard you were on the warpath today."

Good news always spread quickly in the Heart family.

"And your point?" he asked as he dried his legs.

"Cole, darling. There you are," Virginia Heart called. "I have someone I want you to meet."

Her heels clicked on the tile of the poolside area. If he'd told her once, he'd told her a thousand times that high heels and wet tile didn't go together.

"Mother, please be careful."

"Oh, you're such a worrywart. I've been walking on my own feet for sixty-two years. I'm perfectly fine. I'd like you to meet Andrea Delhaven. She's Senator Delhaven's daughter."

His mother stepped aside and presented a cover-model beautiful woman. Yet another one. Cole sighed. Virginia beamed as the introduction was made.

Cole wanted to be polite. He just didn't have it in him right then. He shook the woman's hand. "Pleased to meet you. Excuse me."

He brushed past all three astonished women and snatched up the cell phone he'd left on a chaise. He'd find no peace in his own house tonight, not with his mother and cousin underfoot.

In the dressing room, Cole showered and quickly dressed. Then, without a word to anyone, he slipped out a side door and made his way to the four-car garage, a bottle of Mylanta in his hand.

Taking a swig of the antacid, Cole steered his Town Car toward the tourist area of historic Williamsburg. A night in a hotel room would be preferable to time spent in his own house with his matchmaking mother and his calculating cousin.

Sonja refused to be summoned like one of Cole Heart's flunkies. The entire Heart family had an overin-flated sense of importance. Sure, they were wealthy, but so was Sonja. Sure, the Hearts were influential in the area, even the state, but by no measure was Heart Federated her most important client.

As a matter of fact, for what the company requested and what they were paying, the Heart account had already gotten more than it merited—a whole lot more, as Sonja's vice-president of operations kept telling her. But this job was personal, and Sonja wanted to dot all the I's and cross all the T's—twice.

If Cole Heart wanted to meet with her, he could set an appointment like anyone else. And Sonja had told the ever-efficient Mason just that.

Sonja smiled. He'd probably taken her up on her idea about being a customer in his stores. "And I'll just bet you got a taste of your own Heart experience. I hope it gave you heartburn."

Instead of walking into Cole Heart's office at eight o'clock the next morning, Sonja headed to the weekly meeting of her executive committee.

The operations vice-president started his report with

Sonja's trademark saying. "I've got good news, and bad news."

Sonja reached for her coffee and took a sip. "Bad news first."

Brian Jackson smiled. "Well, it's bad for us, but good for a company in Minneapolis."

Sonja sat up fast and darted an anxious gaze around the table at her three most trusted employees, people she was proud to call friends as well as colleagues.

"Calm down, Sonja," Brian said. "It's not one of us."

Good-natured chuckles around the room eased her. Being preoccupied with Cole Heart had her on edge these days.

"So, what's the news?" she asked Brian.

"Micah Adams is leaving. He's taken a position as manager of product content for an on-line investment firm."

Sonja nodded. "Good for him. Party and send-off?"

Renita, the employee relations vice-president, glanced at her planner. "Two weeks from today. Five o'clock."

Sonja made a notation in her electronic planner, then looked at the group. "And the good news would be?"

Brian glanced around, then smiled broadly as he plopped a thick sheaf of papers in the middle of the table.

"The Robinson account. It's ours. Signed, sealed, and delivered."

Whoops of joy and high fives went around the room. Sonja's smile was the biggest of all.

"Excellent! That's excellent. Congratulations, Brian and Renita. Good work all around."

Brian beamed.

Sonja rose and addressed the group. "For the last

three months, we've been in neck and neck competition to land this account. As you know, Robinson's convenience stores are on practically every other block in the country." She reached for and held up the contract. "This revenue is going to be staggering."

Cheers around the room filled Sonja's ears, and she loved it. Her company made its money by evaluating the business climate for companies, as she had for Cole Heart. Through a network of about two hundred professional evaluaters known as mystery shoppers and a full-time work force of thirty-five, The Pride Group offered assessment, evaluation, market comparison, and for companies requesting the additional services, diversity and customer service training.

Steady growth and careful planning kept the eight-year-old firm on solid financial ground. Sonja believed in rewarding her people for good work. News of landing the Robinson account meant the fat cash bonuses Sonja had promised the executive group if they pulled it off would be a reality. She wanted to take care of the rest of her people, too.

"Can we afford to give everyone a paid personal day?" she asked Janice, who oversaw the finance division.

"Everyone? Like all the full-timers?"

"And the interns," Sonja said.

Janice nodded. "Just so you know, the cash option would be cheaper and less of an administrative headache."

Feeling generous, Sonja waved a hand. "Let each person choose." And it was done. Everyone around the table grinned.

The rest of the long meeting went by with reports from the executive group members about their respective areas. Brian's report about staff operations took the biggest chunk of time as he gave a summary of active accounts, each known as a shop. The group discussed the shops on an as needed basis. Listening attentively, Sonja weighed in with questions or kudos where warranted.

"There's the unfinished business of the Heart Federated Stores," Brian said.

"I'll close that one out," Sonja piped up before anyone could say anything.

Renita glanced at Brian, who shrugged.

"I met with the CEO yesterday and presented the findings. He wasn't pleased." Sonja said. She didn't even try to keep the smile from her voice.

Renita and Brian exchanged glances again.

"Anything else?" Sonja asked the group.

When no one offered anything else, Sonja called the meeting a wrap.

Half an hour later, she stood in her office overlooking the Hampton River. The boats docked at the marinas and the serene view of Hampton University should have calmed her, but they didn't. Her nerves were frayed.

A quick four tap, followed by a two count rat-a-tat on her door, let her know Brian stood on the other side.

"Come on in," she called over her shoulder.

The soft whoosh of air let her know he'd entered.

"Congratulations," she told him.

"Thank you."

"I knew you could do it," she said, finally turning to him.

"You gave me the shot."

Itching to prove something to himself and to her, Brian had practically begged to handle the negotiations on the Robinson deal. Sonja knew that if she hadn't been distracted by Cole Heart, she'd never have given

Brian the leeway to work as he did. The Pride Group was small enough, and Sonja cared enough to be in on every major deal. As it turned out, Brian's involvement was probably for the best. He'd given the account one hundred percent. Being honest with herself, Sonja knew the Robinson people wouldn't have gotten her best work.

"Headed to Jamaica or Bermuda with your bonus?" she asked.

"Only if you'll agree to join me."

Sonja sighed and turned back to gaze out the window. "Brian, let's not go there now, okay?"

She took his silence for acquiescence.

"Do you want to tell me what's going on with this Heart Federated shop?"

"No."

Brian's eyebrows rose. "Okay," he said slowly. "You do know that we've expended considerable resources on a job with marginal return. They didn't even request half the stuff we've done. Are we going to bill them for all of the time and effort?"

"No."

Sonja stood at the window behind her desk, staring at the river and at traffic crossing the bridge leading to downtown Hampton.

Brian sighed. He came around the desk and stood next to her.

"What's personal about this Heart account? You're not telling me something."

"It's nothing, Brian. I'm just working, already. Okay? That's what we do here."

"It's a dead end account," he said. "Yeah, they have eight stores, but they don't want anything but this. You

said so yourself. Since when do you get so involved in
a little pissant account like that?''

"Since now, all right? I'm handling it.''

She turned toward him and caught the hurt expression on his face before he masked his feelings. In recent
months it had become increasingly difficult for Brian
to separate his business acumen from his attraction to
Sonja. Sonja knew the blame for their current personal
situation fell at her feet, but right now she had so many
tugs on her time and her thoughts that she couldn't
deal with this part of Brian.

"It's me, honey. You know you can talk to me about
anything.''

"Don't call me 'honey,' Brian. I've told you that
before.''

He let out an exasperated sigh, then rubbed his eyes.

"I just want to help you,'' he said. "You've been tense
and irritable, not yourself for the last few weeks. I'm
not the only person who's noticed or who's worried
about you.''

"I'm fine. I'm fine. I'm *fine.*'' Sonja gritted her teeth
in an exaggerated smile. "See?''

"Yeah, I see. That's what worries me.''

After Brian left, Sonja sat at her desk staring at her
door. She wondered just what others saw in her these
last few weeks.

She knew she wasn't fine, as she claimed—far from
it.

Sonja Pride, businesswoman, entrepreneur, survivor,
had become obsessed. The only way to get rid of the
obsession was to eliminate the problem.

Her gaze fell to the telephone. She reached for the
receiver and started dialing the number of Heart's corporate office. The fact that she knew the number from

memory made her pause. A chill ran through her, and she rubbed her arms.

Before the first ring, Sonja replaced the receiver.

She was where she was today, doing what she did, because of Cole Heart and his family. None of them knew that, of course. They wouldn't have cared if they *had* known. That's just how they were.

Her animosity toward the Hearts had started a long time ago. . . .

Sonja had enough money to buy her mom the pretty, silk scarf. She'd saved almost a dollar a week by not buying milk at lunch. Even though her mother never said anything, Sonja knew they were poor. She'd learned not to ask for the expensive jeans and sneakers that the other girls wore to school. Her clothes were always clean and pressed, even if they weren't quite in style.

Once she'd seen her mom crying. It frightened Sonja. Her mother was strong, and everything was safe in her arms. But when Sonja asked about the wet tracks on her face, her mom simply wiped at her eyes and held her arms open for Sonja. The big hug made everything better.

She smoothed one small finger down the soft fabric. This scarf would go perfectly with the blue dress mom wore to church sometimes, but so would the red one.

"May I help you, little girl?"

Sonja smiled up at the clerk. "I'm thinking about this scarf. It's for my mom."

The Heart Department Store clerk smiled at her, then looked at the price tag. "It's pretty, isn't it?"

Sonja bobbed her head accordingly.

"Do you have enough money?"

"Yes, ma'am. I've been saving up. Now I just have to decide which one."

The clerk smiled at her again, and Sonja knew she'd made a friend.

"Well, my name is Marie. I'll be right over there. Call for me when you decide, okay."

"Yes, Miss Marie."

With another smile for her, the clerk headed to a display of Easter hats.

Sonja's consideration of the scarves continued for several minutes. Her mind made up on the blue one, she glanced around for Miss Marie, then reached for the delicate material.

"Just hold it right there, you."

Sonja froze and gripped the scarf in a suddenly tight hand.

When she turned around, she saw that the shrill voice belonged to an older lady with wrinkles around her mouth and pin curls so sharp you could cut a finger on them.

"I've been watching you. Did you think you were going to steal that today?"

Sonja's eyes widened, and she released her hold on the scarf. "No, ma'am. I'm going to buy—"

But the woman cut her off. "Security alert. Security alert."

Sonja's frightened gaze darted around the area. Several people had turned to stare. "No, you don't understand. Miss Marie—"

A burly security guard appeared out of thin air and grabbed Sonja's arm. "All right, little lady. This way with you."

"But I didn't do anything."

"Yeah, yeah. That's what they all say," the guard said as he escorted her away.

But not before Sonja heard the wrinkled saleslady tell another patron, "Just like their kind. Trashy. Always looking for a way to take something that doesn't belong to them."

Squirming in the security guard's grip, Sonja turned to get another look at her accuser. The woman smiled and a chill ran through Sonja. Again she looked for the nice Miss Marie, but didn't see her.

The guard led her to a small office in the back of the store, where she was questioned for half an hour. Then her mother was summoned from work. The surprise was ruined, and her mom had lost wages when she had to come get Sonja. . . .

The shrill ring of the telephone startled Sonja. Blinking several times, she glanced around. She wasn't in a Heart Department Store. She wasn't eight-years-old. She didn't stand erroneously accused of trying to steal.

She was thirty-three years old, and about to pay the Hearts back for that first of many indignities.

# Chapter 4

Cole Heart was in a rage, and fit to be tied. Mason ran after him in an ineffective attempt to get him to sign off on some capital requests. But Cole wasn't in the mood to allocate any resources to any Heart store.

If he hadn't needed prior approval from his board of directors, he would have shut down three of the company's eight stores until the respective management teams could get their collective acts together.

In his fake beard and glasses he'd ventured into two more Heart stores. His experience in the Hampton store hadn't rated any postcards home, and the Richmond store left him practically apoplectic. The rest rooms in the mens' department and in the customer service areas wouldn't qualify as clean, but filthy. The mirrors, full of scum and smudges and who knew what else, hadn't been washed in what looked like months. The floors looked as if a rugby team had run amok on them.

He'd been shortchanged twenty dollars when he

paid for a pair of sneakers. And a clerk—one of his employees!—actually told him to "go kiss off" when he'd mentioned a sale item being cheaper at a competing department store. Her response *should* have been to ask the customer to bring the ad in for an additional five percent off an identical product at Heart.

"Mason, where the hell is my—"

She jammed a blue bottle of Mylanta into his hand before he finished the sentence. Cole unscrewed the cap and took a deep swallow, then secured the top.

"Did you take your blood pressure medication today, Mr. Heart?"

His quelling look told Mason where she could put her idea.

"I thought you were getting Sonja Pride in here today."

"She was tied up. You have an appointment for eight-thirty Friday."

Cole slammed the Mylanta bottle on the edge of his desk. He missed, and the plastic bottle bounced to the floor. Mason picked it up and placed it within reach in the middle of his desk.

Snatching up his desk phone, Cole asked for Sonja's number.

Mason called out the seven digits as she headed for Cole's private dressing room and bath. She returned to him with one hand held out and a glass in the other.

"Why isn't she answering?"

"I couldn't say," she told him. She held her open palm in front of his face.

Cole rolled his eyes but plucked the small pill from her palm, then accepted the glass of water and downed the medication.

"Happy now?"

"Ecstatic," she said, a touch of a smile at her mouth.

"I thought these people were a reputable outfit. Why isn't anyone answering? Hello? Sonja Pride, please. This is Cole Heart from Heart Federated."

He waited impatiently for the receptionist to put him through. Mason kept trying to put a pen in his hand so he could sign the paperwork, but Cole wasn't having it.

"Later," he said, waving her away.

She sighed and retreated.

Before he could huff again, Sonja was on the line.

"Good afternoon, Mr. Heart."

Cole wasted no time getting to the point. "My plans have changed, and I'm going to our Detroit stores a day early. I know it's inconvenient, but I'd like to meet with you. Tonight, if possible," he added.

"Mr. Heart, it's already five o'clock. I have an engagement at seven."

Cole looked at his watch, then reluctantly conceded to himself that there were people who actually stopped working at five.

"I realize it's late in the business day. And I promise not to keep you overly long." He had to push the next words out of his mouth. "I wouldn't be calling if I didn't need you."

Luckily for him, Sonja Pride didn't make him actually beg. With the caveat for him to make it quick, she agreed to meet him at six.

Cole's need for Sonja took a decidedly personal bent the moment he saw her walking across the lobby to the enclave. Through the glass wall he watched her, and the completely foreign notions of desire, jealousy, and possessiveness whipped through Cole so fast that he almost staggered as he stood at the door waiting for her. She walked like a harem dancer, and Cole wanted to possess her.

He shook his head to clear it. The dress. It had to be the dress. The red material was practically molded to her body. The hem stopped right above her knees. The woman's legs went on forever. Her bare arms and shoulders beckoned to be touched. She'd swept her hair up and back in an elegant evening style.

Cole wanted her. He wanted to be the man she'd shimmied into that dress to impress. He wanted to be her seven o'clock appointment.

He held the glass door open for her.

"Good evening, Mr. Heart."

She looked like sin on a mission, but she was all business when she greeted him.

He shook hands with her. "This way," he said. "We'll meet in the boardroom."

When she turned, Cole's breathing stopped. The smooth golden brown of her bare back beckoned his hand. He took a deep breath to steady himself. Then, without a word, he led her to the conference room in the center of the corporate enclave.

A large oval table was surrounded by deep leather chairs. Paneled walls gave the room an inviting, stay-a-while atmosphere. On a far wall hung a large portrait.

"My assistant made a pot of coffee before she left a few minutes ago. May I get you a cup?"

"No, thank you. I'm fine."

"Have a seat, please."

Sonja placed her attaché case on the marble tabletop, but continued to stand. "As I said earlier, I don't have a lot of time. What is it that you need?"

Cole was pretty sure she didn't really want to know.

Putting some distance between them, Cole walked to and opened a wall cabinet to reveal an enlarged map of Virginia, North Carolina, and Michigan. For a moment he contemplated the areas marked by red hearts. Then he turned back to her.

"I did what you suggested. I shopped three of the stores as a customer."

"And?"

He walked to the table and rested his hands on the high back of a chair. "And how do I know those so-called employees I met weren't your plants, put there to prove your claims?"

From across the table he saw her eyes narrow.

"Are you challenging my integrity, Mr. Heart?"

For a long, tense moment, they stared at each other. Then Cole's heavy sigh filled the large room. He felt as though the weight of the world rested on his shoulders.

"No, Ms. Pride," he said quietly. "The only thing I'm trying to do is keep my company in the black."

The rare moment of candor surprised him. He glanced at her and saw that she, too, looked momentarily stunned. Quick as a flash, Cole stood erect.

"Two people were fired, six put on probation. Another four were disciplined."

"All that from just walking into your stores as a customer?"

"I'm not sure I'm up for what I might find in Detroit."

"Is that why you're going early?"

He nodded, pulled a chair out from the table, and sat in it. Sonja slipped into the rich leather seat closest to her. From across the table he contemplated the portrait hanging on the wall behind her.

"Word has gotten out that heads are starting to roll.

I'm expected in Detroit for a meeting Tuesday, so I'm sure everything will be shipshape by Monday. My plan is to visit the stores tomorrow and Sunday."

Sonja nodded. "And what, exactly, is it you needed from The Pride Group?"

Cole ignored the question and asked one of his own. "Do you shop at Heart, Ms. Pride?"

"No."

His dark brow slanted in a frown at her flat, almost militant answer.

"Why not?"

"Because I don't go to a business to be treated like a second-class citizen. Heart has operated like that for . . ." She paused, taking a moment to regroup. "I choose to spend *my* hard-earned money in businesses and establishments that value me as a customer. A lot of consumers are like that, Mr. Heart. If I want to be harassed, I don't need to pay for it with cash or with a Heart credit card."

Cole stared past her again, and was silent so long Sonja turned to see what kept his attention.

"The stores haven't always been that way," he said. "A long time ago, a Heart Department Store was the place to go. Now, I'm afraid, we're turning into dinosaurs."

He got up and went to the oil painting. From the corner of his eye he saw her swivel her chair around to track him.

"That's my grandfather, Coleman Heart the first. He founded the first store, a dry goods shop for colored people in Newport News. He gave Negroes credit when few other merchants would. He eventually leased and then bought another building. By nineteen fifty he had three stores. Everyone in the family worked in the business."

Cole stared at the portrait, then shook his head in disgust. "Now, the only thing this family is unified about is greed."

Sonja leaned forward. "I'm sorry. I didn't hear the last part."

Cole turned, and for a moment seemed surprised to see her sitting there. The look vanished in a flash. "Nothing. I was just talking to myself."

Sonja's distrustful expression told him she suspected she'd missed something significant. Uncomfortable with the fact that he'd let himself slip up like that, Cole squared his shoulders and then faced her again.

Sonja crossed her legs and cleared her throat.

Cole's mouth went dry. The woman's legs were magnificent.

She glanced at her watch. "Thank you for the history lesson, but what does that have to do with The Pride Group?"

"This isn't a history lesson, Ms. Pride. It's what I do. It's what I am."

"Well, I'm sorry to hear that you define yourself by your job. I'm sure that works for you, though." Sonja stood up. "Mr. Heart, I told you I have an engagement this evening. If there's no point to this meeting, I'll be leaving now."

He glared at her. There was a lot to dislike about this woman, but Cole had done some homework—enough to know she was highly regarded, had a national client base, delivered on her promises, and had played a major role in turning around some businesses for the better. He didn't like it one bit that he had to reach out to her, but Cole wasn't about to cut off his nose to spite his face.

"I want you to help me turn things around at Heart," he said. "I read your portfolio. I'm interested in having your people come in and help my people set things straight. I have the vision. The training from your outfit can help me maximize my goals."

"May I ask you a frank question?" she said.

"What?"

"Why are you such a hardass?"

That brought him up short. He stared at her, hard. And again, Cole was reminded that Sonja Pride was all woman—just the kind he'd like if he had time for foolish entanglements.

"You don't pull any punches, do you?"

"Why should I? I don't have anything to lose."

"What about losing my business?"

Sonja shrugged. That gesture told Cole a lot; mostly, that she could take him or leave him. To a man accustomed to having people jump when he said "Go" or drop when he said "Sit", Sonja Pride presented a unique experience. Rarely were his views and commands met with opposition, let alone indifference.

She intrigued him.

She didn't seem to care that he was CEO of a major retail company in the region. She seemed downright unfazed by his glares, stares and direct attempts at intimidation. As a matter of fact, the more he pressed the more she seemed to relax.

Cole wondered idly what it might be like to press her firm body against his. Not generally given to lascivious thoughts, Cole let himself run with the notion of getting close to this woman. Slender but not skinny, Sonja had curves in all the right places, curves that Cole realized he hadn't taken time to notice on other women in a long time. Or maybe other women didn't have them like Sonja Pride. Something about this woman scrambled him.

"So," he finally said, "you don't care if I take my business elsewhere?"

"Mr. Heart—"

"Call me Cole," he said before he thought to stop himself.

She lowered a brow at him. "*Mr.* Heart, the assessment of your department stores did not require an extensive outlay of resources from The Pride Group."

"So what you're saying is that I'm small potatoes, and you couldn't care less."

Sonja's soft chuckle rippled through Cole like a whispered promise. A slight tremor ran through him. He recognized it as sudden, inexplicable desire for this hard-edged businesswoman with the honey-gold complexion and the oh so tempting curves.

"Do you play poker, Ms. Pride?"

"Very well."

His gaze traveled over her, then finally met and searched her eyes. Cole didn't know what he searched for, but he seemed to have found it in Sonja. Such an attraction could prove perilous to his concentration and his bottom line. With his company on the brink of disaster, now was not the time for distractions, particularly the kind she presented.

In Sonja he saw a quiet danger—or was it desperation?—and a simmering sensuality. His soul recognized a survivor, a kindred spirit, while his body craved the challenge of her.

"I think I'd like to sit down at a poker table with you one day."

"You'd lose," she said matter-of-factly.

"I think not. But we'll save that debate for another day."

Sonja's deliberate contemplation of the slim, gold watch on her wrist didn't escape Cole.

"I'm keeping you from your engagement."

"Yes, you are."

"Why don't you like me?"

"I beg your pardon?" she said.

The open hostility riding above her awareness of him intrigued Cole. As a matter of fact, he was downright fascinated by it. He sensed another level of emotion brewing just beneath her not-quite-genteel veneer. Like a craftsman stripping away the cheap veneer covering an exquisite piece of wood, Cole wanted to strip Sonja of the many layers he sensed in her.

"I asked why you don't like me."

"Liking or not liking you has nothing to do with this conversation, with your company, or with the way I run my business. I'll take under advisement the fact that you want additional services from The Pride Group. I'll have Brian Jackson, my operations vice-president, give you a call. He'll assess your needs and then determine the feasibility of a continued business relationship."

"No flunkies, Ms. Pride. I want you overseeing the job."

"That won't be possible." Sonja snapped shut her attaché case. "*If* there is a job," she added.

And Cole found himself dismissed.

After he watched her walk away, Cole realized exactly why he was attracted to her. It wasn't the body, and it wasn't the dress. Cole liked sparring with her. Not many women shot back with the same level of intensity he dished out.

Cole smiled, and long-neglected face muscles protested the action. Then he laughed out loud, making a sound that hadn't been heard in an even longer time.

Sonja fought a losing battle to keep her attention focused on working the room at the reception. Her every thought and every breath included Cole Heart's face and physique.

She accepted a glass of white wine from a passing waiter and smiled a greeting at someone who waved to her from a distance.

Something totally unexpected had happened while she talked to Cole Heart in his big conference room. Sonja had tried to refuse to let the vulnerability she heard in his voice soften her heart, but it had slipped in, anyway. She'd seen Cole Heart, as a man who deeply cared about his company, not as a calculating, bottom-line businessman. They had that in common.

Sonja wanted to maintain her anger at him, but instead she'd found herself wanting to smooth his brow. She'd first viewed his dark blue, tailored suit as a crutch he used to bolster the intimidation factor he'd so finely honed. But watching him move about the room, Sonja realized he wore the clothes simply because they looked good on him.

Too good.

So good that she'd spent more time thinking about helping him out of them than she'd spent on getting out of the room and to this social commitment.

"Sonja, you look captivating, as always. So glad to see you, darling."

Sonja exchanged an air kiss with the owner of a local PR firm. For a while now, Ted Gallòne had been trying to convince her that they should join forces and merge their businesses. Sonja remained uninterested.

"Good evening, Ted."

"Magda has thrown another fabulous bash."

They looked around the crowded hotel ballroom. The party honored all the corporate donors who'd contributed to a community-wide volunteer program.

"Is Brian here?" Ted asked.

"He should be. But I haven't seen him or Renita."

"Ah, Renita. A lovely woman."

"She's still married, Ted."

He clasped a dramatic hand across his chest. "You wound me, Sonja."

"Yeah, yeah," she said, chuckling.

"Oh, there's Dr. Jamison. Excuse me, please." With that, Ted disappeared into the throng.

Sonja shook her head, then sipped from her glass and moved in to mingle. But even as she worked the room her thoughts were never far from the man she'd sworn to hate.

They were two Type A personalities, two high D's on the personality indicator tests. Sonja knew Cole Heart posed a significant danger, not to his company or to hers, but to Sonja's own rock-solid equilibrium.

If somehow, in some impossible way, they found themselves together, they would clash and burn like Mount Vesuvius in its ancient volcanic glory. The passion would burn hot and wild and glorious.

Sudden need gripped her and Sonja jerked, tense. Wine sloshed in her glass. Sonja darted an anxious gaze about the room, vainly looking for a distraction, for anyone to get her mind off the track on which it seemed to be stuck.

She couldn't—wouldn't!—allow anything even remotely sexual to ever occur with him. But her body had already primed itself for the fire dance with Cole Heart. Sonja wanted to feel him wrapped around her, strong, tight, and hard. Once in her head, the image wouldn't leave.

Her obsession with Cole had taken a turn for the worse.

She wanted a piece of his hide, all right. But this time the promise of fulfillment had nothing to do with her revenge agenda, and everything to do with an intimate liaison.

# Chapter 5

*One week later*

Sonja now realized she'd made a major tactical error in handling the Heart account herself. She should have passed it off to someone in Brian's division, taken status reports, and rejoiced in the Heart family's misery.

But the Heart case was personal, and now she found herself paying the price for letting Cole Heart get under her skin. Sonja's nerves, tight as a bowstring, had reached critical mass. No one, not even Brian, dared venture into her office, where she prowled and growled like a lioness in heat.

Cole didn't fare much better. He swept through Detroit kicking butt and taking names. And now, he faced his angry board of directors. Board members had been taking calls all week about Cole's swath of destruction through the stores.

He wasn't in the mood to be trifled with.

"Cole, your behavior has been an abomination," Justine Heart declared as the others milled about the conference room.

"This company has gone to hell, and I aim to reverse that trend," he told his aunt.

"How dare you!" Justine fumed.

"Now, boy. These ain't the old days," said Uncle Jimmy, who stood within hearing distance. Uncle Jimmy wanted to be called James, but no one ever did that. He claimed to be hard-of-hearing, but he had been hearing what he wanted to for the last fifteen years.

Cole reached for a large mug in front of his place at the board table. To the casual observer, he drank from an oversized cup of latte. Only Cole and his secretary Mason knew he downed a health food store concoction designed to settle his stomach.

He rapped a small gavel on a square block. That got the attention of his mumbling board members.

"If everyone will take a seat, we can begin."

"I want to know the meaning of the outrage that's been going on in the stores for the last two weeks. I got a call from—"

"Aunt Justine, we'll get to that in a moment."

With an iron will Cole took control of the meeting. He got through the assorted reports and projections without much debate, but storm clouds drew in when he reviewed the company's bleak financial outlook.

First quarter profits were down by thirty-eight percent from the previous year. Projections for the second quarter, which included the traditionally heavy bumps of Easter, Mother's Day, and graduations, were not at all rosy.

Of course, Justine Heart was the first to speak up. "I,

personally, find it very difficult to believe that in the course of nine short months the stores have gone from profitable enterprises to losing propositions."

"That's what I've been saying, Aunt Justine. It didn't happen in nine months," Cole said. He nodded to Mason, and the lights in the room dimmed as a projection screen lowered. In moments, graphs charting the company's revenue and expenses were before the assembly.

"As you can see," Cole said, using a laser highlighter to review each area, "this decline has been evident for the last twelve years. A number of significant capital projects—"

Jimmy cut him off. "All necessary," he said as he chomped on an unlit cigar. "We had to keep modern."

Nods around the table let Cole know the battle would be all uphill.

Cole had expected this reaction. Undaunted, he continued. "As I said, a number of significant capital projects as well as remodeling at several stores has drained profit potential. We cannot afford to continue in this manner—"

Justine butted in. 'Well, I think—"

"Hear me out, please."

Justine huffed but kept silent for the moment.

"A solution, at least a partial one, is at hand," Cole said. "We need to return to our roots. Return to the principles on which this company was founded—customer service and community focus. We've strayed too far from the mission."

"Jim Crow doesn't exist anymore, Cole. It's a new day. Hell, it's almost a new millennium."

"That's right, Aunt Betty. And my aim is to carry Heart Federated into the new millennium as a strong, vital player in the retail industry. We can do that by making our customers the focus.''

At that, a couple of heads around the table began to nod. Cole was finally making some ground.

Then Mallory spoke.

"Cousin, are you saying that *we* are somehow responsible for the lackluster first quarter revenue?'' Mallory's manicured hands swept open, encompassing the twelve other people at the table. "It would appear that mismanagement and lack of focus is to blame for these numbers we're seeing.''

"Now, Mal, the boy did inherit some problems,'' Jimmy muttered.

*Problems you helped create,* Cole impotently fumed at his uncle.

"Be that as it may,'' Mallory said, "he's had ample opportunity to affect change.''

Cole gritted his teeth. "Mallory, I would hardly call nine months ample opportunity.' ''

She smiled sweetly. "That's because you've wasted so much time harassing the help and throwing money at consultants.''

Not for the first time, Cole wanted to strangle his cousin. They'd been bitter rivals since their days of sharing a playpen. Mallory felt that she, not Cole, should have been given the helm of Heart Federated after Cole's father died.

Cole's succession to the CEO's chair had been anything but smooth. Ever since, Mallory, his deceased uncle's only child, had used every available opportunity to get a dig in, to undermine Cole's authority, and to make his life hell in general.

Mallory was a beautiful woman. Most of her victims, including those sitting at this very table, were blinded by her looks and never knew what hit them when she struck. And they always seemed reluctant to believe that pretty Mallory could do anything wrong. But Cole knew the face of his enemy, and had enough knife wounds in his back to be wary and always on the offensive with his cousin.

He smiled at her. "I'm glad you mentioned consultants, Mallory. I have here for everyone the report from the one your mother recommended we use." Cole's lethal smile lit on Mallory even as she gave an exasperated look toward her mother, Justine.

Justine shrugged and sat back. "What now, Cole? And does this have something to do with you firing Millie James's daughter? Whatever am I going to say to her when we meet for bid whist?"

"It has everything to do with our former employee Millicent James," he said.

Cole nodded to Mason, who started a slide presentation about The Pride Group's report. By the time he finished, indignant and outraged sputters filled the room. Then he related his own experiences in the stores, and the hubbub grew louder as everyone spoke at once.

"I don't believe it."

"Lies, all lies."

"Who did you say this outfit is?"

"How do you know they're not working for the competition?"

"Cole's right," Lance said from where he sat between his parents. "Have any of you guys *been* in one of our stores lately? They look and feel like mausoleums."

Glances and shrugs around the table told the story of the family's neglect.

"Well, I was in the Virginia Beach store a couple of months ago," Justine said. "I needed a lipstick. I had a wonderful Heart experience. Each member of the sales staff I encountered was courteous and impeccably dressed."

"Of course you had a wonderful experience, Justine. They know you pay their salaries," Bev Heart Smith said dryly.

Cole hid a smile and sat back in his chair. "Where do you shop, Aunt Justine?"

She looked affronted. "What do you mean?"

Cole nodded toward her. "That suit you're wearing. Where did you buy it?"

"In Paris, of course."

"Um hmm," Cole said. "And you, Aunt Betty, that lovely peach dress. Did you get it from one of our stores?"

"Don't be silly, dear. This is from Nordstrom."

Cole looked to the ceiling for guidance.

"Is anyone in this room except me wearing or carrying anything from a Heart store?"

No one, not even Mallory, met his telling stare.

"*I* am, Cole," Lance said. "This suit, the shirt, and the socks. The tie is from Saks."

Cole stood and walked behind each of the chairs. "So, what we have here are eight supposedly wonderful stores that practically no one in this family ever sets foot in or shops in. What does that say about our commitment to the bottom line? What does that say about our stores?"

"Is there a point, Cole?" Mallory asked. She got up to refresh her drink. Plucking a bottle of carbonated water from an ice tray, she twisted the top. For a moment, the only sound in the room was the fizz and hiss of the water. "I hardly see how where we purchased the clothes we're wearing has anything to do with the bottom line. A line, by the way, that's slipping into red ink every day."

Cole whirled around and pointed at her. "It has everything to do with the bottom line, Mallory. If you, with your M.B.A., can't see that, what did they teach you at your fancy business school?"

"They taught me how to see through the smoke and mirror tactics produced by desperate executives who hope to divert attention from their own shortcomings and failures." Mallory took a sip of water and smiled. "Learning that was worth the price of admission."

Cole counted to ten and wondered if he'd taken his blood pressure medicine that day.

"Did they also teach you how to recognize barracuda?" he said. "I'm told that sometimes the species will attack itself when it sees its reflected image."

A couple of snickers could be heard around the table.

"Children, play nice," Uncle Jimmy warned.

Cole turned away from Mallory and back to the people at the table. "We digress," he said.

"As usual," Mallory added dryly as she took her seat. "I believe that's your specialty."

That was the last straw. Cole lost his patience.

"Look, Mallory. The rest of us come to these meetings because we have a sincere interest in the long-term viability and profitability of this company. You come to tear down and pick unnecessary fights. You're still pissed off because you're not in charge. Well, grow up and get over it. As long as I'm head of this company, I'm going to do everything in my power to make it a top-notch retail establishment. If that includes pointing out the deficiencies that detract from the profit margin, I'm going to do it. If it means firing insubordinate clerks and inefficient managers, I'm going to fire them. If it means asking the very legitimate question of why Heart family members don't shop in their own stores, I'm going to ask it. I'm in charge, and that's my job.''

"We'll see for how long," Mallory shot back.

Justine slammed a bony hand on the table. "Don't get too big for your britches, Coleman. You may control a considerable interest in this company, but it is by no means a controlling interest. You were voted into that chair's seat, and you can be voted right on out.''

Mallory jumped up. "That's a splendid idea, Mom. I make a motion that Coleman Alexander Heart III be ousted from the chairmanship of Heart Federated Stores, Inc., on the grounds of failure to produce on promises made, squandering company funds on needless and expensive so called, fact finding consultant fees, and being a general pain in the ass.''

"I second the motion," Justine chimed in.

Cole exploded. "Wait one goddamn minute.''

The room erupted in shouts, accusations, and name-calling. Mason backed her chair up to get out of the line of fire as papers and angry words went flying in every direction. Justine lunged for the gavel at Cole's place.

Afraid she meant to do someone bodily harm with the piece of wood, Lance wrested it from her hands and found himself tussling with his aunt.

It took Uncle Jimmy's shouts to bring order to the room.

"Everybody just shut up!" he hollered above the fray.

So rare was the occasion when Jimmy asserted himself publicly that the room fell silent. Jimmy Heart was a behind-the-scenes player, not given to outbursts. Everyone stared at him.

"Is this a meeting or a prizefight? How about we act

like grown-ups here? Mallory, sit down. Cole, get over here. Everybody sit down."

The cousins glared at each other, but did as Jimmy commanded.

"I remember the day when this family was on one accord," he said. "How did we get to this point? This is pathetic, absolutely pathetic. Mallory and Cole, both of you have been trying to prove you're capable of running this company. If this kind of behavior is your example, I think we need to entertain that proposal from Knight and Kraus and get a real management team in here."

"I like that idea," Justine said. "I make a motion—"

"Shut up, Justine," Jimmy interrupted. "We don't need any more of your motions. Your instigating has caused enough problems."

"Don't you talk to me that way."

Jimmy pointed a finger at his sister-in-law. "Not another word, Jussie."

A few people around the table exchanged surprised glances. Jimmy, usually a behind-the-scenes, go with the flow man, was apparently fed up.

"Thank you, Uncle Jimmy, for bringing order to this meeting," Cole said as he stood to reclaim control of his meeting.

"I'm not done yet. Sit down."

Cole sat.

"Knight and Kraus is a good company," Jimmy continued. "This family has put a lot of years into these stores. But maybe it's time for us to sell out and take the money from an outfit that will do a good job with them. It'll get rid of a lot of stress and let us all do some other things."

Murmuring bubbled up around the table.

"We've already decided that route isn't the most expedient," Cole said.

His authoritarian moment now passed, Jimmy Heart took his seat, hunched his shoulders, and sat back.

"We can always *un*decide," Mallory said.

Bev Heart Smith spoke up. "Cole, I have a suggestion."

Cole glanced at his half-sister, then at Lance, who shrugged, telling Cole he didn't know what his mother's suggestion might be.

"What is that, Bev?"

"First, Mallory's motion needs to be rescinded."

Pointed looks turned toward Justine and Mallory. The older woman huffed.

"Jussie," Jimmy's rumbled warning silenced her.

"My motion may have been made in frustration and anger, but it remains an issue we need to discuss," Mallory said.

"Not today," Jimmy said, ending the debate.

Mallory rescinded her motion to oust Cole, then militantly sat back.

"Thank you, Mallory," Bev said. "My other suggestion is that we table the discussion about the chairmanship and selling to Knight and Kraus until the next board meeting."

"Excuse me," Mason said.

All heads turned toward the secretary sitting to Cole's left.

"Yes, Mason?" Cole said.

"There's a presentation from the chamber of commerce and the merchant's association scheduled for next month's board meeting."

"Well if we're going to discuss and vote on selling to

Knight and Kraus, we don't need to meet with them. That can be canceled," Mallory said.

"I agree," Bev said.

Cole sighed inwardly. His half-sister represented his strongest ally on the board. If he couldn't count on her and her family, he would really be in trouble.

"We pressed for that meeting," he reminded the board.

"Well, Mason can just tell them that something has come up," Justine said.

"I really don't think we should rush into anything," Cole said. "Six more months should give us a better—"

"Cousin, do I need to remind you about those excellent skills of yours?" Mallory asked.

Cole's glower should have cowed her, but she glared right back.

"Mallory's right on this one, Cole. No need to delay the inevitable," Uncle Jimmy said.

Cole wanted to refute the statement that defeat was inevitable, but he knew when it was time to temporarily retreat. He'd have to work the individual family members, and sway them to hold off.

Heart Federated, his grandfather's legacy, meant too much to him to let it all go without a fight. Four weeks wasn't a lot of time. Could he turn things around in a month? Cole wasn't sure if he could, but he knew he'd give 250 percent in an effort to save the company and his grandfather's dream.

A few minutes later he adjourned the meeting. It hadn't gone at all as he'd anticipated, but with his family he should have known better. Bev and Justine sniped at each other on the way out the door. The others grumbled and formed little allegiances that Cole knew he'd have to overcome. It went without saying that Heart phone lines would burn hot tonight.

Uncle Jimmy just shook his head and lit his cigar. "Hell of a mess, Cole."

With that summation, Jimmy took his leave.

Before long, just Cole, Lance, and Mason remained in the boardroom. Lance popped open a can of Coke and sat down while Mason gathered financial statements left on the table by some of the relatives.

She cast sympathetic eyes at her boss as he wearily dropped into one of the leather chairs.

Cole sat back and closed his eyes. "Well, that went well."

"Don't worry, Cole. It'll all work out," Lance said.

"Yeah, if I kill myself. Or better yet, I should kill Mallory."

"You shouldn't even joke like that," Lance said. "It's bad for your blood pressure. By the way—"

"Yes, I took the pill. Get off my back, will you? The two of you are like mother hens."

"Someone has to look after you," Mason said.

With the papers stacked, she went to the wet bar and filtered hot water through the coffeemaker. Then she brought a large mug to the table and put it before Cole.

"It's chamomile tea. It might help you relax."

"I hate tea, Mason."

"I know."

Cole opened his eyes and saw more than the two people in the room with him. Her short answer said a lot. Cole realized the concern Mason and Lance showed meant they genuinely cared about him. He couldn't say that about a lot of people. Cole had always been a loner. The few friendships he'd developed were more business associations than true friendships. In college he'd had

a few friends and mentors, but they were people he'd
lost touch with through the years.

He sighed, recognized the truth in his mother's constant nagging. The fact of the matter was Cole *didn't*
really have a life outside of his work. And now, his guard
had been up so long that he found himself lashing out
at the very people who had his best interests at heart,
people who would be his friends if he opened up.

Cole knew he gave Lance a hard time, but he was
preparing his nephew, grooming him for the day when
he'd control a significant part of the company.

He'd lost control of his meeting and his temper today,
two things that had never happened to him before. For
too long, he'd been burning the candle at both ends.
His blood pressure and his constantly upset stomach,
which he now suspected might be an untreated ulcer,
were testimony to that.

"I'm sorry I snapped at you, Mason. Why don't you
two head home? It's been a long, unpleasant day. I'll
finish up here."

Lance and Mason exchanged glances. Lance
shrugged and got up. "That's just how Mallory is. You
know that. She's always been a climber."

Cole nodded. Mason gathered her materials and
headed to her office.

"Well, I'll see you tomorrow?" Lance said.

Cole nodded again and stared at a point beyond
Lance. Then, with thoughts turned inward, he didn't
see or hear Lance leave.

After a few minutes, Mason poked her head in the
conference room door. "Drink the tea, Mr. Heart."

"I will."

She smiled and said goodnight.

Long after everyone had left, the quiet of the enclave

surrounded Cole, but the silence didn't bring peace. Cole sat in the empty boardroom with his hands steepled on the table. He believed in Heart Federated, the company founded by his grandfather and practically bled dry by his father and uncle. Cole leaned forward and studied the portrait of the family patriarch as if divining wisdom from the image in oil.

His father and Uncle Jimmy had left a mess, and Cole, stuck with cleanup duty, would need a miracle to fix everything before he got fired.

He rubbed his eyes and sighed, then went to stand before the painting.

His whispered entreaty came from a fear-filled place deep inside him. "Pops, I'm in trouble. Tell me what to do."

# Chapter 6

"Cole, Justine is having about three kinds of fits. Whatever did you say to her at that meeting? Of all the nights for me to miss."

As he ate lunch with his mother the next afternoon, Cole couldn't help wondering if he could count on his own mother's unconditional support if the board actually moved to oust him. He'd gotten about four hours sleep, and wasn't in the mood to rehash the disastrous meeting. But he also knew his mother wouldn't be put off.

"The whole meeting started on a bad note, and got progressively worse."

He recapped the highlights in about five minutes.

Virginia Heart sipped her Bloody Mary, then shook her head. "What Mallory needs is a man and some babies."

Cole closed his eyes and prayed for deliverance. His mother's answer for every professional single person, him included, was to find a nice man or woman and settle down. Now that she'd hit on the topic, it would take her five, four, three, two—

"Speaking of which," Virginia sequed.

Cole sighed in resignation.

"You weren't very nice to Andrea Delhaven. She's in town for a meeting and a little relaxation. I told her you'd love to show her around."

"Mother, please do not add appointments to my calendar without consulting me."

Virginia frowned. "That's your problem, Coleman. This isn't an appointment. It's a date. I don't think you know the difference. Andrea is a lovely girl. She came out of Wellesley, you know."

"I don't care if she came out of the South Bronx. I don't need you—"

"Watch your tone, young man. You might be head of the company, but I'm still your mother."

Cole apologized, but couldn't find true contrition in his heart. His mother had been flinging debutantes and socialites in his path for the last four years. He'd grown sick of the meddling. If he thought it might help, he would tell her he was gay. But he knew how well Virginia Heart could roll with any situation. She'd just say, "Oh, why didn't you say so?" and then head off on a search for the perfect man for him.

"Mother, it's about all I can manage right now to keep Heart afloat. I don't have time for social entanglements."

Virginia waved a hand. "So we'll sell it. It's an albatross, anyway."

Cole wanted to scream in frustration. Didn't anyone understand? Was he the only Heart who felt the company was more than a source of profits that financed luxury living and country club status? Heart Federated was about product and people and service. Why was that so difficult for everyone to grasp?

"I would like some grandchildren before I pass on," Virginia persisted.

"You won't be passing on anytime soon. Besides, you have Lance."

Virginia rolled her eyes. "I don't have Lance. You do. He used to stop by the house a couple of times a week. We'd talk or watch television or see a movie. But now, he doesn't have time. He's always at work. Watching him is like watching you all over again."

Cole masked his hurt with a question. "And being like me is so terrible?"

Because he didn't indulge her every whim, he was always considered lacking in his mother's eyes. He'd never been the son Virginia had envisioned, somehow never lived up to the unspoken expectations she had. After thirty-five years, he thought he was over it.

She dabbed her mouth with the linen napkin. "Oh, you know what I mean. Lance's entire focus is the company. The two of you need to learn how to live. There's more to life than the bottom line."

Cole gave up. The argument wasn't a new one. And he never won. Ever.

"Andrea is a lovely girl. She's twenty-six, has never been married, knows Washington like the palm of her hand."

When Cole didn't say anything, Virginia prodded. "So, are you going to see her? She's staying at the Lodge for the next few nights before heading back to Northern Virginia."

He gave her the best answer he could. "I'll see if I can fit it in."

Virginia didn't look at all satisfied.


Sonja found herself compelled to see him. She shouldn't be interested in the enemy, and the flaw in her character that drew her to him didn't sit well with her. But Cole's image haunted her. Not the mental photograph of a hard-nosed, hard-hearted business-man, but one of an all too human man who did his best to make the right decisions for his company and his people.

She pulled harder on the rowing machine at her spa and girded herself with memories of why this mission was so important, why she couldn't allow herself to get soft. . . .

"Life isn't always fair, honey," her mother said.

Ten-year-old Sonja didn't want platitudes. Her new dress was ruined. She'd been so proud of the pink and white creation. Next to the start of school in the fall, Easter was the only time she got a completely new outfit from a department store.

The pretty dress she'd donned this morning was now splattered with grime. She and her mom had come downtown to get her picture taken. A coupon for a free portrait had lured them to the Heart Department Store. They'd just gotten off the bus, and before they could even enter the store a big car came to a stop at the curb, splattering standing water from the spring rain all over the left side of Sonja's new dress.

She flashed stricken eyes at the car, then at her dress and back at the car. The laughing faces of a boy and a girl in the back seat of the big car stayed with her. They thought it was funny that she'd been doused with the dirty water. Sonja's lower lip quivered.

"Miss, are you all right? Here, this might help."

Sonja accepted the handkerchief from a young man in a blue suit. He looked toward the car, where the children still sat laughing and pointing.

"Some people have no manners," he told Sonja's mom. "Is there anything I can do?"

Busy trying to keep from crying, particularly in front of the rich kids in the fancy car, Sonja couldn't answer.

"No, but thank you for your help. We'd come to get a picture taken, but we'll just go home now," her mother said. "Come on, sweetie. We'll wait for the next bus over here."

The young man dug into his pocket then whistled for a cab. "Ma'am, I'm sorry about what happened. Let me at least get you a cab, so you don't have to wait."

Sonja's mother wouldn't accept the money from the young stranger, but she did thank him. As the first tears began to fall, Sonja watched him frown at the children in the car before heading down the street. Then her attention turned to a woman coming out of the store.

A big hat with dangling white teardrops first caught Sonja's eye. The lady's white suit matched her shoes and handbag. That's what rich looked like. An older man laden down with packages hurried behind her. The packages were stored in the trunk and the woman stepped into the car. As it drove away, Sonja saw the license tag: Heart 1.

"That's one of the owners of this store," her mother said.

"Well, her kids and her driver aren't very nice," Sonja sniffled. "What am I going to wear to Sunday School tomorrow?"

Sonja's mother looked at the ruined pink dress. "Well, we'll see what I can do when we get home."

The likelihood that the dress could be saved wasn't very good. The lady in white could probably buy another dress for *her* daughter, if one got ruined. Sonja and her mom didn't have that luxury.

"It's just not fair," Sonja said. . . .

"Girl, what are you trying to do, row across the Atlantic or something?"

Sonja blinked and looked up. Her neighbor and workout partner Ann stood next to the rowing machine. She took a sip of water from her bottle as Sonja stopped rowing and got up.

"I get into my workout," Sonja said by way of explanation.

"It looked as if you were out to get even with somebody."

Sonja shrugged. "Yeah, well. Whatever. Your aerobics class finished?"

Ann nodded. "What bee bit your butt?"

Shaking out her arms and legs, Sonja shrugged. "I just have a lot of things on my mind lately."

"You work too hard, sisterfriend."

Sonja smiled. "Keeps me out of trouble. Ready to run?"

"Let's roll."

Sonja liked jogging outdoors. Breathing the fresh air cleared her thoughts and her lungs. But today, as always of late, her thoughts remained crowded by a big man with stormy eyes.

By the time she got back to her office in Harbour Centre, Sonja was ready to leap tall buildings. But she wasn't ready to deal with Brian, who waited for her.

"I'm back," she called as she breezed through the entryway.

"Did you remember to eat while you were at lunch?" her secretary asked.

Sonja grinned and held up an apple. The secretary shook her head.

Brian hurried beside her. "Hey, chief. Got a minute?"

"Sure," she said as she accepted phone messages. "Let me get settled. Fifteen minutes."

Sonja flipped through the three slips: one from her mother, one from Ted Gallòne, the PR guy, and one from Cole Heart. Sonja's heart raced, and her fingers suddenly felt tingles.

"Get a grip," she coached herself as she dropped her briefcase on a round table and made her way to her desk. She knew her mom had called to confirm their weekly dinner date. Whatever Gallòne wanted could wait.

According to the message, Cole had called about fifteen minutes ago. Sonja settled in her chair and stared at her telephone.

"He's just a client, just a client."

She dialed his number and was put right through to him.

"Thank you for calling me back so quickly," he said.

Sonja held the telephone receiver out and stared at it a moment. When did Cole Heart get polite?

"Not a problem. How can I help you?"

"I know you said you'd have one of your people take a look at our situation, but something has come up. Ms. Pride, I really could use your expertise. I'm on a very tight timetable. I respect your judgment, and would like to talk to you face-to-face. This isn't about mystery shoppers at the store. It's much more complex now, and I need your help.''

Sonja cleared her throat. He was asking a lot, but his need struck a chord with her. Sonja was really curious about his new problem and what motivated him to act like a human being.

"Let me check my planner." From her purse, Sonja pulled her electronic date book. "How soon did you want to get together?"

"Whatever works for you," he said.

Sonja raised an eyebrow and stared at the telephone. "What, no barking orders about 'Now!'?"

The brief noise on the other end of the line might have been a self-depreciating chuckle, or it could have been a curse. Sonja couldn't tell, but the sound made her smile.

"I'm turning over a new leaf," he said.

This time, Sonja did the chuckling. "Well, this I want to see. Do you know where the Lighthouse Restaurant is?"

"It's a couple of blocks from our Hampton store."

"I'm pretty jammed the rest of the week. If tonight is okay with you, I'll make reservations for eight."

"Thank you," he said.

"Not a problem." And she meant it.

Sonja arrived at the restaurant first. She requested a large table with good light, and was escorted to an ideal spot that featured an excellent view of the waterfront marina. She placed her purse, planner, and laptop in a chair and slipped into her seat to wait for Cole.

He arrived within two minutes.

"I'm sorry to have kept you waiting," he said as he took his seat.

"I just arrived."

The server took their drink orders, rattled off the night's specials, then disappeared.

"You have me quite curious, Mr. Heart. What's your crisis?"

Cole stared at his menu, then looked Sonja directly in the eyes. "I have thirty days to save Heart Federated."

"What happens in thirty days?"

"My board will take a vote to sell the company to outsiders."

"Why are you telling me this? You don't know me. You don't know anything about me."

"Yes, I do," he countered. "Your firm was recommended by someone I respect—most of the time," he added from the side of his mouth. "I've seen and read about your work. I've talked to some people. I was impressed by the thoroughness of your presentation. In hindsight, I should have had you present your findings to the Heart board of directors. It might have gone over better."

"What happened? Were you faced with a room of skeptics?"

"To say the least."

"Look what it took to convince you," she said.

Whatever Cole planned to say was cut off by the server, who arrived with their drinks and was ready to take their orders. Sonja ordered sea scallops and gulf shrimp with fettuccini and sun-dried tomatoes. Cole opted for the house specialty, jumbo lump crab cakes. Their seafood orders placed, Sonja reached for her laptop and powered it on.

"What do you want from me?" she asked.

"A miracle."

Sonja smiled. "You're going to have to be a little more specific."

Cole sat back in his chair. "Are you familiar with the history of Heart Federated?"

Sonja knew more than she wanted to, but to avoid answering she reached for her water goblet and made a noise that could be interpreted either way.

Cole leaned forward and smiled. "It's always been a family business. I told you it was started by my grandfather, Coleman Heart. He worked until he was eighty, even though my father took over the chairmanship in the early nineteen seventies. My father and my Uncle James ran the company, my dad as CEO and Uncle Jimmy as CFO, for almost twenty-five years."

"And you took over nine months ago."

Cole nodded. "Right after my father died."

"The news reports said he died at his desk."

A shadow crossed Cole's face. He sat back in his chair. "Yeah. My mother found him."

Sonja had never considered the human side of the Hearts, but she supposed they bled and grieved like everyone else. She reached a hand out to him. "I'm sorry. I didn't know that. She must still be grieving."

"No need to be sorry. He died doing what he loved. And he left my mother a very rich woman. She's fine."

Sonja sat back and crossed her arms. If he wanted to take a cavalier attitude, that was just fine with her. She actually preferred that he keep his distance and cease dropping his guard long enough for her to peek inside and get curious.

"So what's happened in the time you took over?" she asked. "You mentioned there's talk of a buy-out."

Cole stared at her, wondering how much to say—

how far he could trust her. In one regard, his cousin's criticism was right on the mark. He'd relied on empirical data for so long that he'd stopped listening to his gut. That internal gauge had carried his grandfather through his entire career, and it used to guide Cole. These days, though, he didn't usually have time to get quiet and reflective. Right now, something about Sonja Pride told him she could be trusted, that she was a woman of integrity.

"There's been a power struggle going on from the moment my father died," he said. "Years ago, interest in the company was chiefly divided among my grandfather's four children—my father and his two sisters and brother. There's some minor interest owned by people outside the family, but it's scattered, and amounts to about ten percent of the total. The bulk remains with family members. Through deaths, marriages, and what have you, Heart Federated has remained in the extended family, but no one single person or family has controlling interest."

Sonja nodded. "That's not so unusual. I'm still not hearing the part about how The Pride Group factors in."

She reached for the breadbasket on their table. Tearing off a piece and buttering it, she saw him watch her hands and then track their movement to her mouth. Sonja tried to ignore the heat that swirled through her at the thought of Cole's intense energy directed her way. She met his gaze for a moment.

Something electric passed between them.

Sonja licked her lips, then forced herself to focus on business. Cole cleared his throat.

"I want you to help me convince the board members that Heart is a company worth fighting for, that its future can be as a retail giant in this market and the other markets where we have retail outlets.''

Keying in a quick notation on the laptop, Sonja nodded. ''So you're talking about a market analysis, some comparative statistics, maybe a survey of long-time as well as new customers?''

''Exactly,'' Cole said. ''I can turn this thing around. When my board members see the promise and the potential of Heart, they'll get on board, so to speak.''

''And if they don't?'' she asked.

# Chapter 7

A muscle flicked angrily in his jaw.

"Failure is not an option, Ms. Pride."

"Hmm," was all she said in response.

"Could I have been mistaken about your ability and reputation for making things happen? I only deal with the best."

His expression and his tone held a note of mockery that Sonja didn't appreciate.

"If memory serves correctly, and it does, Mr. Heart, I'm not the person who begged for this meeting."

"I don't beg."

Sonja shut her laptop just as the server brought their dinners. "I really don't see the point in continuing, Mr. Heart. We get along like oil and water. The services of a public relations firm may be more in line with what you need and could use."

"Are you saying I need to work on my bedside manner?"

Distracted enough, she didn't need any images of beds and Cole.

The waitress looked from one to the other "Uh, what's your pleasure?"

"We're leaving—" Sonja said.

"We're having dinner," Cole said at the same time.

Wisely, the server remained silent while the strong willed couple stared each other down.

Cole backed down first. "You're right. But oil has its purpose, just as water serves its own." He extended a hand toward her. "Please, stay."

Puzzled by his abrupt change, Sonja pushed the laptop out of the way, then nodded to the server.

The woman let out a barely audible sigh, and placed their meals before them.

Sonja and Cole ate quietly for several minutes, the only sound between them the clink of silverware on china.

"Have you always been so bossy?"

Cole paused as he reached for water. His chuckle broke the tension between them. "As long as I can remember. I believe the experts call it being assertive."

"Men are assertive, and women are bitchy."

"I wouldn't characterize you that way."

Sonja bit. "How would you, then?"

"Goal-oriented. Thorough. Intense." When he looked at her, Sonja would have sworn she saw another adjective in his eyes.

She had a few choice adjectives to describe him. But for some reason her favorite ones—overbearing, arrogant, self-centered—didn't quite ring true. She was starting to see a different side of Cole, a side that made her wish they'd met under other circumstances.

Sonja sat there rehashing her anger, going over the

foolproof plan she had to assist him in his downfall. Not wanting him to see the turmoil that raged in her, she glanced away.

Buying time, she sipped from her glass. Then, finally, a decision. She met his direct stare.

"What is it you want The Pride Group to do?"

And that ended the negotiation between them, sealing their pact to work together. Sonja knew she could get more info to aid her cause by working in his camp rather than outside it. They spent the rest of their dinner, dessert, and coffee brainstorming strategy. Sonja took notes on the laptop. Occasionally, they got so animated they forgot they were out in public.

Sometime later, Cole suppressed a yawn behind an open palm.

"It's not the company," he said, excusing himself. "It's been a long twenty-four hours."

"I have an early day tomorrow," Sonja said.

They fought over who would pick up the check. When neither would graciously give in, they settled on dutch treat.

"You make it difficult for a man to be gallant," he told her as he saw her to her car.

Sonja wasn't about to get into that territory with this man. She found him attractively intriguing. The quiet Hampton night was too serene, too lush with expectation. Her own traitorous thoughts, running along the lines of chivalry and romance with Cole Heart starring as the knight, made her cling to a shred of indignation. Unfortunately, right now, Sonja couldn't quite recall what she had to feel indignant about.

"This is a business arrangement, Mr. Heart. I don't expect you to be gallant. Gallantry is for other types of relationships."

Cole studied her. "I disagree."

Sonja opened her mouth to answer, but Cole put a halt to the rebuttal.

"Let's save that fight for another night. I'm beat, and you might win if we go there now."

Sonja cocked her head, regarding him with a trace of amusement. "And losing, of course, would be a fate worse than death."

Cole nodded. "I don't lose."

Sonja smiled as she slipped into the driver's seat of her gold Lexus. "We'll just see about that."

Cole's reaction and playfulness surprised her. So did the smile that spread across his whole face. He wore it easily, and she found herself enchanted.

The warmth of his smile echoed in his voice. It stayed with Sonja long after she'd driven away. It stayed with her in the shower she took before bed, and it stayed with her as she lay nestled between the sheets of her very large, very empty bed.


Two days later, Cole's assistant ordered dinner for four, then left Sonja and Cole closeted in Cole's office with Lance and Brian. They hammered out a plan that had enough of Cole's input for him to feel comfortable with it. All that remained was a delegation of duties and the timetable.

Eventually, Lance and Brian called it a night, leaving Cole and Sonja to the final details.

Sonja bit into an egg roll and looked at the list of ideas on a flip chart.

"This is six months' work, Cole."

"We have less than four weeks."

"You're not being reasonable about expectations," she said.

"The Pride Group isn't up to it?"

She turned on him. "We're up to whatever you pay for. My people aren't the concern here. A lot of this depends on the cooperation of your general managers."

"They'll be on board, or they'll be out of jobs."

"Vinegar isn't always the best way to catch flies."

Cole poked chopsticks into a cartoon of Moo Goo Gai Pan. Before he could answer her, his office door flew open.

"There you are, dear. I figured you were working late as usual, so I brought Andrea by."

Virginia Heart blew into the room like a gale. Sonja looked up and caught her breath. The woman's ivory raw silk suit and matching, wide-brimmed hat reminded her of the Heart woman from so long ago. For a moment, Sonja was transported back to her childhood. The anger, hurt, and embarrassment bubbled up, and she forced herself to tamp it down.

This had to be the same dramatically dressed woman who'd swept into the car that had ruined her Easter dress.

This was Cole's mother?

"Mrs. Heart, I'm sure he's busy," the casually elegant beauty said.

"Good evening, Mother. Ms. Delhaven," Cole said.

Mother? Who in the world called their mother Mother? Did ice run in his veins? Delhaven? As in senator? Lightning fast, the questions raced through Sonja as she rose to greet the two.

Sonja took another look at the woman with Cole's mother and decided it was, indeed, that Delhaven family.

Cole made the introductions. If he heard his mother's sharp intake and then stricken look when Sonja was introduced, Cole didn't show it.

He turned his attention to the work he and Sonja had been doing before the interruption and completely missed the dismayed look on Virginia's face. But Sonja saw it. Then, with grace, she took in the silent snub from Virginia, who refused to shake her hand.

"This is Andrea's last night, Cole. You promised to show her around."

Glancing at his watch, then at Andrea and then Sonja, Cole's gaze finally landed on his mother. "Well, it's rather late."

"Cole, don't feel obligated on my part. I live in Northern Virginia, not Northern Alaska. I can come back some other time. It's just a few hours up the interstate."

While Andrea was being gracious, Sonja watched Virginia noticing the assorted take-out boxes and cartons.

"Don't tell me the two of you ate all of this."

Cole sighed. "The others left, Mother. We were just going over some more details."

"Details about what?" Virginia asked. Then, before Cole could answer, she waved the question away. "Never mind. I'm sure I know. Well, since you obviously don't have time to entertain guests," she said, looking pointedly at Sonja, "I suppose we'll leave. I'm sorry, dear," she told her own guest.

Andrea shook Sonja's hand again, saying, "It was a delight meeting you." Then she turned to Cole. "Maybe on my next trip, we can plan something. Or you can come up to Arlington."

With another frosty glance in Sonja's direction and then a pointed stare at her son, Virginia Heart swept out of the office, with the senator's daughter following.

"You can say it." Cole invited after they left.

"Say what?"

"My mother is a drama queen."

The hint of a smile threatened at Sonja's mouth. "I wouldn't say anything of the sort."

"Well, you can think it."

A small smile escaped this time. "Actually, I was thinking she seems quite concerned about you."

"In more ways than one," Cole said dryly, dismissing the line of conversation. He turned his attention back to their project.

Sensitive to all slights that winged her way from Hearts, Sonja wondered if the presence of *any* female would have resulted in the cold shoulder from Virginia Heart, or if somehow it was meant specifically for her. Since she'd never met the woman, Sonja came to a logical conclusion: If Virginia Heart's job in the company was to train employees in customer service, the woman had succeeded in making them rude imitations of herself.

Once again assured, she settled into the job at hand.

Twenty minutes later, their heads almost touched as they sorted through options. Sonja glanced up, and her breath caught.

The small sound made Cole look up.

They'd ostensibly been working on the account objectives, but Sonja saw the questions in his eyes and the promise she knew radiated from her own. With Cole Heart it would be hot and wild, tender and sweet.

Time stopped moving. Electric tension charged the room as they stared at each other.

Sonja's gaze searched his eyes while Cole's dipped to her mouth. They leaned forward, scant inches separating them. For a breathless moment, they remained still, anticipation humming between them. Then Cole's head angled, and Sonja's eyes drifted closed.

With a jerk, Sonja yanked back. She got up.

Her heart raced a mile a minute. She'd almost kissed him! "Uh that, I . . . we . . . I think we're done for the night," she finally got out.

Cole sat back and watched her hustle about, gathering notes and keeping her distance.

"Ms. Pride?"

Sonja swallowed deeply, then turned to face him. "Yes?"

Slowly he rose. It took Sonja a full thirty seconds to realize he held something out to her.

"Your calculator."

She snatched the instrument from him, careful not to touch him. "Thank you," she murmured.

Cole cleared his throat. Sonja, perturbed with herself, glanced around to make sure she'd gathered everything.

"I suppose the next thing you're going to say is you'll have Brian Jackson call me."

Sonja slipped the thin strap of her compact saddlebag over her shoulder, then clutched her ever ready laptop to her breast.

"No, Mr. Heart. What I planned to say next was, and is, goodnight."

She made haste out of his office, not realizing until she got outside and to her car just how much time they'd spent alone. Together. Did he feel the same heat she did? Could he possibly know how much she craved the feel of his mouth on hers?

Not until much later did two things dawn on Sonja. First, she'd genuinely enjoyed working with Cole. She liked the way his mind worked. She also liked seeing the potential of a project develop first on paper and then in reality.

Her own prejudices aside, Heart Federated Stores had that potential. The company teetered on the brink of either boom times and wild prosperity or wretched extinction. Its future depended on how aggressive a campaign they wanted to wage, how willing the players would be to the bottom line, at whatever the cost or sacrifice.

The second thing Sonja realized: As founder and president of The Pride Group, she had well-trained and well compensated people who could and should have been doing the work she'd done tonight. But, she thought, smiling, she didn't mind one bit. Working in the trenches from the ground up on a project afforded a unique opportunity.

"To study corporate methodology and strategy," she told herself. *Yeah, right,* her conscience answered back. *Okay. So I got a little personally involved. No biggie.*

The upshot? Sonja looked up and found herself more than a little personally involved. Tonight, she'd brought Brian more as a shield than as one of her vice-presidents. But having him in on the planning had also served another purpose: It gave Brian the opportunity to see inside the Heart enclave and to realize that Heart Federated wasn't a pissant account to be dismissed out of hand.

What Cole proposed was going to cost him.

It came as something of a surprise to Sonja to realize that the money her company would earn on this job didn't rate as high on her list as the personal satisfaction part. She enjoyed the work she did, and ultimately, that's what mattered most. In recent years, the more the company expanded the less opportunity she'd had to actually *do* the thing that gave her the most joy—interacting with her customers, shining a spotlight on their flaws, and turning those blemishes into highlights and achievements.

"You're the boss. Delegate to yourself, and do what you want to do."

Sonja smiled as she brushed her teeth, then critically regarded her face in the wide mirror over her vanity.

What she *really* wanted to do was kiss Cole Heart.

As he swam laps in his pool that night, Cole was having similar thoughts about Sonja. He'd spent the entire meeting wanting her and wondering about her relationship with that Brian Jackson fellow. More than once he'd caught the man ogling her with more than business on his mind. Cole recognized the signs and the look, because he'd been guilty of the same himself. Picking up those vibes from the competition, a rival who knew her better and probably intimately, didn't sit well with him.

Cole thought about the kiss that wasn't. He tagged the wall on the deep end of the pool and pulled himself out of the water. His erection grew as he walked to the pool room. The very thought of her lush mouth wrapped around him made him fervently wish she hadn't pulled away.

Something about that moment had frightened her.

Cole grabbed a towel and flung it over the door of the bath stall. He stepped into a very cold shower, but it did little to ease the want. Sonja Pride was trying to keep their relationship on a strictly business level, but Cole had other ideas. She'd wriggled in under his

defenses, made him take notice—even if unintention-
ally.

His mother flaunted beautiful, well-bred, and educated women in front of him all the time. Not a single
one of them, including the senator's daughter, had
piqued his interest or his libido in the slightest. But
sparring with Sonja Pride made him heavy and aching,
with want.

He smiled. Cole Heart *always* got what he wanted.

# Chapter 8

"Well, you were right," Brian said. "How'd you know that initial shop for Heart would lead to this contract?"

Sonja didn't know anything of the sort, and wasn't particularly in the mood to talk about Cole with Brian. She'd spent a tumultuous night tossing and turning in her bed, alternately dreaming about Cole and fantasizing about making love to him. The last thing she needed on her mind today was Cole and his stores.

She aimed to change the subject.

"Anything I need to know about the Robinson account?"

Suspicion clouded his eyes. "What is it with you and this Heart guy?"

"Excuse me?"

Brian rose from the chair he'd been lounging in in her office and dropped the Heart file on her desk.

"Sonja, you've been blowing me off this account for weeks now. What's the deal? You pay me to make things happen around here. If you're withholding information that will help my people do their jobs better, I need to know about it."

Feeling guilty now, Sonja turned her back on the view from her window and faced him. "It's not you, Brian. And I'm not holding anything back," she lied. "I've had a lot of things on my mind."

She reached for her coffee and took a sip. It had grown cold.

Brian saw her frown and headed to the coffeemaker Sonja kept in her office. He brought the carafe to her, then topped off her cup and his own.

"Thanks," she murmured. Then, too cheerfully, she said, "I've been thinking—"

"Uh oh, that usually means more work for me and my division.

Sonja smiled. "Not this time."

Brian settled in his chair again and Sonja leaned against the edge of her desk.

"So what's the thought?"

"I'm having fun again."

He sipped from his mug and regarded her. "When did you stop having fun?"

"I don't know." Sonja tested her answer and realized she spoke the truth. She didn't know when it had stopped being fun. "All I know is that coordinating those Heart shops, making plans with Cole, getting into the brainstorming process, all that stuff just jazzed me."

Brian lips twisted into a cynical smile. "Cole? Are you sure it's not the man who has you 'jazzed', as you say?"

Sonja looked at him. "What are you saying?"

Brian put his cup aside and leaned forward. "I'm saying that ever since you got involved with this Heart shop, I've been getting the cold shoulder. I don't like it."

Sonja put her own cup down and stood up. Brian did, too.

"I've told you before, Brian. We can't mix business and pleasure. I'm not ready for, or interested in, a relationship."

He stepped forward, crowding her space. "That's not what you said that night."

Ducking away from him, Sonja moved to the table in her office and turned her back to him. *That* night was a mistake, Brian. We got caught up in the moment."

"It was more than that, and you know it."

His arms snaked around her waist and she yelped. "Stop it!"

Brian dropped his arms, moved back a step, and narrowed his eyes at her. "If this is the part where you're playing hard to get, I'm not getting into it."

Sonja folded her arms and stared him down. "Listen to me, and listen well. I'm not *playing* anything. We do not have a relationship. I am not interested in a relationship. I value your work here. I admire your talent for getting employees motivated. I applaud the numbers you bring in. I'm proud of you and your team for landing the Robinson account. But I am not your girlfriend, your lover, or your woman. Is that clear?"

Cold resentment turned his face into a mask she couldn't read.

"Very."

"Good," she said.

A moment later, her office door slammed behind him.

Sonja cursed.

She ran her hands through her hair and cursed again.

This was not how she'd planned to spend the morning.

Her telephone line buzzed a moment later. Sonja reached over and punched the speaker button. "Yes?"

"Ted Gallòne for you. He says he's been trying to reach you."

Sonja sighed and fell into her chair. She picked up the receiver. "Hello, Ted. I'm sorry I didn't get back to you the other day. Nice seeing you at the reception the other night. What can I do for you today?"

"Sonja, darling. I was starting to get a complex. I thought you were avoiding me."

Sonja nodded her head. "Of course not. What's up?"

"I have an idea for you," he said.

"Ted, we've talked about this before. I'm not interested in a merger."

"Darling, hear me out before you shoot me down."

Sonja smiled. Ted could be a pain, but he was a good PR man despite the 'Darlings' and his worn-out 'You look fabulous.' "Okay, shoot."

"Let's collaborate on a project," he said.

"What kind of project?"

"Cross training. You take some of my people for a project and I'll take some of yours. At the end we compare notes, see how things worked, then look for other efforts where our talents and strengths could be cross-utilized."

"Why?"

"Why what?" he asked. "Sonja, darling, you're the best at what you do. I'm fabulous at what I do. Our worlds are always colliding. You know that's true. Why not make the most of it? Can't you see the beauty of the proposition?"

Right now, the only thing Sonja was seeing was a

headache forming. Tugging open a drawer, she dug out a bottle of aspirin. She checked the expiration date and frowned. The container went into the trash. She reached for her electronic datebook and made a notation to buy some Tylenol or Excedrin or something.

"I don't know, Ted," she hedged.

"I have a project in mind."

*Of course,* she thought. *Now we get to the real deal.* "What's that?"

"Heart Department Stores."

Sonja sat up. How did he know The Pride Group was working with Heart? All of her mystery shoppers were sworn to secrecy. They weren't supposed to ever let anyone know what they did, or where.

"Why Heart?" she asked.

Ted laughed. "Have you been in one of those stores lately? Have you seen their TV spots? Hideous, just hideous," he declared.

Sonja agreed, but she wasn't about to tell Ted that. "Have you worked up a presentation?"

"Oh, I have some things cooking, darling. A little stir-fry is starting to sizzle."

Sonja had a sudden need to know exactly what Ted Gallòne was up to. "How about lunch today? Twelve 'o clock. Someplace downtown."

"Excellent, darling. I'll meet you at Rigby's."

Sonja bit back her protest. Of all the restaurants, he would choose the one she hated. "Fine. See you there."

No sooner had she hung up with Ted than her phone buzzed again.

"It's Renita," her secretary said. "One of the shoppers has been busted for shoplifting."

On days like this, entrepreneurship wasn't all it was cracked up to be. Sonja rummaged in the trashcan and retrieved the bottle of expired aspirin. She popped four of the tablets in her mouth, washed them down with cold coffee, and took the call from her employee relations vice-president.


"You weren't very nice to Andrea Delhaven."

Cole was trying to get some reading done before he had his quarterly meeting with the general managers. His mother's presence in his office was making that extremely difficult.

"I told you before you started that I didn't have time for that. She seems a nice enough sort. I'm sure you two hit it off."

"The point was for *you* two to hit it off."

He held up the report he was trying to read. "Mother. Please. This is the only time I have to get this done."

"Well, you were rude to her."

"I apologize."

The rote apology didn't sit well with Virginia. "Why did you have that woman in your office last night?"

"What woman?"

"That Pride woman."

Cole glanced up. "You know her?"

Virginia looked away and fluttered her hands. "I . . . of course not."

Shaking his head, Cole flipped to the next page of the sixty page executive summary. "She's the owner of The Pride Group. They're the outfit doing the mystery shopping and analysis for us."

"Us? As in the stores? Our stores?" Virginia's voice rose with each successive question. The last one came out a squeaked croak.

"Is there a problem?"

"I, well, now . . . I see." She strode to the table where Mason had left a pitcher of ice water for Cole. Pouring a glass, Virginia fanned herself with one hand and then took a cooling sip of water.

"Are you coming to this meeting?" he asked.

Virginia whirled around. "What?"

Cole closed the report that obviously wasn't going to get read today. "Mother, what's wrong?"

Clearly agitated, she began pacing the area in front of his desk, the long silk scarves of her caramel-colored duster flowing out behind her as she walked.

"You had time to associate with that Pride woman, but no time to entertain someone who at the very least might be a good ally in Washington. You've been muttering about opening a store there, yet you rebuff the very person who might be of some help in that area. Andrea is an asset, not to mention a very lovely girl."

Would every person under forty remain a boy or a girl in his mother and uncle's viewpoints?

"I don't want assets for friends, Mother. Assets are for the bank balance and the stock portfolio."

"How would you know the difference? You don't *have* any *friends.*"

The barb hurt, particularly since it was true. He was developing a friendship with Sonja Pride. Didn't that count? Cole reached into a drawer in his desk and pulled out his blood pressure medication.

"Thank you for that glowing assessment of my life."

"Why must you always pick fights?"

Cole was sure he'd have tossed her out of his office by now, if she weren't his mother. He twisted the cap on the brown pharmacy bottle and shook out one of the pills.

"You know, if you spent more time out in the world

and had the occasional date, you wouldn't need those pills.''

"Next time I see him, I'll tell my doctor that."

"I don't know where you got such a sarcastic attitude."

Cole had a few ideas, but prudence in this case was the better part of valor. Funny how sparring with his mother gave him a headache, and sparring with Sonja energized him.

The thought of Sonja made him smile.

"What?" Virginia asked.

He raised an eyebrow in question.

"Why are you smiling all of a sudden?"

"Is that against the law?"

"You never smile. You never laugh. Cole, you never *live.*"

"That's probably because I'm so busy trying to make sure everyone in this family will be able to afford the luxuries they've grown accustomed to."

"I should hope you're counting yourself in that number, young man. That house of yours and those suits you wear aren't exactly pauper's quality."

Cole glanced at his watch. "I have ten minutes before the quarterly manager's meeting. Is there something specific you wanted today, or did you just drop by to say hello?"

"You're my son, Coleman, but sometimes, I swear, you try my patience."

He wisely remained silent and schooled his expression to remain neutral.

"And as a matter of fact, yes. I came to find out why you were fraternizing with that woman."

"If you mean Sonja Pride, I told you. Her firm comes

highly recommended. I've hired her to help us get things turned around before the vote."

All the color in Virginia's face drained away. She swayed on her feet, and Cole dashed to her side to steady her. He led her to a chair and poured another glass of water. "Are you all right? Should I call your doctor?"

"I'm fine. I just . . . . highly recommended by whom?"

Cole was busy taking his mother's pulse and watching her color. She yanked her hand from his arm. "Stop it. I'm fine. I'm fine. Who recommended her to you?"

"Aunt Jussie. She said—"

Virginia's shriek of outrage drowned out the rest of Cole's answer.

"That no good, battle axe instigator. How dare she!"

Virginia was up and out of the chair before Cole could make heads or tails of what had set her off. In a flurry of silks and profanity, she was out the door, calling her sister-in-law Justine everything but a child of God.

Cole let out a frustrated sigh. Whatever that was about was sure to take another year off his life when his mother finished with it. He slipped on his jacket, picked up a legal pad, and headed to the small conference room off his office for the meeting, which he could only hope would be more productive than the time he'd just spent with his mother.

# Chapter 9

Sonja liked to give back to the community whenever she could, so she made cash donations, hired interns, and volunteered time to causes she believed in. For weeks she'd been looking forward to Community Volunteer Day, a day set aside for business and professional people and concerned citizens to help out where needed. For eight hours, she'd paint and clean up and forget about problem employees, calculating PR types, and the man who haunted her dreams and her days.

She left her electronic planner, her laptop, her cell phone, and even her pager in the trunk of her Lexus. There would be no distractions today, no intrusions. She'd relax and have some fun with the other volunteers while they worked on their assigned cleanup project.

At city hall she boarded one of the buses that would shuttle them to their worksites. Sonja recognized lots of the people, from city council members and local clergy to current and former clients. Gone were the power suits and all the trappings of their professional worlds. In sneakers, cutoff blue jeans and a white tunic covered by a gray tank top, Sonja fit right in with the sweatpants and jeans crowd.

At the large community center where Sonja and fourteen other volunteers had been assigned, each person got a baseball cap and a painting, weeding, or repairing job. Sonja pulled painting, and went inside to collect her supplies and get started on her rooms.

Still trying to figure out how and when he'd agreed to this, a disgruntled Cole filed off the second bus arriving at the community center. Mason and Lance seemed suspiciously and conspicuously absent when he read the item on his daily schedule. And neither one claimed knowledge about the pair of worn jeans, his favorite Nikes and the Heart Department Store sweatshirt neatly placed in the middle of his desk when he'd arrived at the office at six-thirty. He wasn't amused then, and he wasn't amused now.

With a ton of work to do and a situation brewing at the Raleigh, North Carolina, store, volunteering to paint and clean up a ramshackle community center didn't rank high on his list of priorities.

"Coleman Heart, how nice to see you!" a woman exclaimed. "I didn't think Heart Stores participated in the Community Volunteer Day."

Cole smiled at the mayor's wife and shook her hand. Backing out now wouldn't be a good thing. "We're changing our philosophy," he said. "It's a pleasure to see you again. What's the plan for the next few hours?"

"I can't take the paint fumes, so I'll be out here cleaning up the flower beds and planting. Go ask that young man wearing the red vest what your assignment is."

He turned in the direction she pointed and saw a man hustling volunteers to their assigned duties.

With his tiny cell phone clipped to his waist, Cole didn't feel quite so out of touch with his element. Knowing Mason would call if something came up, he approached the volunteer coordinator, but not before overhearing a surprised exclamation from yet another person who seemed shocked to see him.

"For Pete's sake," he muttered, "you'd think I hadn't lived here all my life."

"Mr. Heart. What a pleasant surprise." The red-vested coordinator beamed. "When I saw your name, I figured it was some other Cole Heart."

Cole was starting to get angry. Had he and the company grown so out of touch with the community that his mere appearance caused a stir?

"What am I supposed to do?"

His bark had the suitably typical effect on the volunteer coordinator, who looked flustered and then dropped his clipboard. Cole counted to ten, wondered about the ratio of incompetents to competents in the world, and waited for the guy to get himself together.

"Uh, you're inside, Mr. Heart. Painting from the left wing. That's the nursery and the classrooms."

"Fine.

Cole headed in that direction.

"Uh, Mr. Heart?"

He turned back and watched the man scurry to him.

"Here's your hat. Thank you for giving of your time today."

Cole looked from the man to the dark blue baseball cap offered to him. Accepting the hat, he adjusted the band width and settled it on his head. Then, with a genuine smile for the coordinator, he said, "Thanks." It was the best apology he had to offer.

The man smiled, nodded, and then turned back to other volunteers waiting for his directives.

Oddly in a good mood now, a whistling Cole strode into the center, picked up an extended length paint brush, and followed the signs to his worksite.

He stopped at the first room he saw.

Ghastly orange walls greeted him. That was the first thing he noticed. The second thing that got his attention was the most phenomenal pair of legs he'd ever seen. A rich golden brown, they were long and smooth and just the delicate shape he liked. And they were attached to a body that made his own take notice.

The woman laughed as she smoothed a paintbrush roller through a tray on the top of a six-foot ladder. "Who in the world thought burnt orange was an appropriate wall color? It's going to take three or four coats to hide it."

"Sonja?"

Another woman chuckled at the comment as they both turned to greet the newcomer. Her cheery welcome and hello should have covered Sonja's gasp of surprise, but Cole heard.

Suddenly in a terrific mood, he stepped into the room with his paintbrush.

"Good morning."

"Wh-what are you d-doing here?" Sonja stammered.

Clutching her roller, she dripped paint on the floor. She looked as if she needed some air. *Good*, Cole thought. That's what she did to him, too.

"Watch out, Sonja. You're making a mess," the other woman said as she approached Cole and extended her hand.

"Hi, I'm Nellie Saunders. I'm usually a nurse over at Riverside, but today I'm painter *extraordinaire*. And on the ladder is Sonja Pride. She's from a local market research group."

Cole shook her hand. "I'm Cole." He pointed to his sweatshirt. "With Heart Department Stores."

Nellie nodded and went back to stirring cans of paint. "Great having you with us. We'll get done faster. Why don't you take that side?" she said, pointing across the large classroom.

The only side Cole wanted was one near Sonja. "If we work the same area and then spread out, everyone will have the same consistency."

Nellie shrugged. "Works for me. What do you do at the department store?"

"He owns it," Sonja said dryly.

Nellie did a double take. "Really? You're a Heart?"

Cole nodded.

"Hmph. I didn't realize any of them lived around here. Well, I have a question for you."

Waiting for the question, Sonja settled on the ladder and smiled at him.

"How come you're always out of off black pantyhose? Have you ever noticed that, Sonja? Every time I go in that store, there are never any available. And that little woman with the attitude who works that department is clueless."

"You mean the store here in Hampton?"

Nellie nodded.

"I don't know. But tell you what—I'll find out and get an answer for you. Do you have a card, or something with your phone number?"

"Not with me. I'll write it down before we leave today."

Cole dug into his jeans pocket and pulled out some change. He handed Nellie a silver heart.

"What's this?"

"It's a Heart token. Employees generally have them. It's good for twenty-five dollars in store merchandise. I'll find out about those pantyhose for you, and in the meantime use that—on me."

Nellie grinned. "As my kids say, groovy, man."

Cole glanced up at Sonja, who gave him a nod of approval.

"And what's with that weird fluorescent light in the womens' rest room, the one across from the fitting rooms? It's like a strobe or something. If I have to go, I go to another store or wait until I get home."

He couldn't answer that question, either, but promised to find out.

The tough questions done, the three settled into an easy camaraderie,

Well, easy for Cole. Sonja's heart had just slowed down from its erratic beat.

"There have to be fifty cleanup sites around the city today. How did you end up here?"

Cole watched carefully as she glided the brush along the two-foot outcrop near the ceiling. Not a problem. This looked easy enough. He stuck his long brush in a tray of paint Nellie put before him. Paint oozed out of the deep end and onto the newspaper she'd placed on the floor.

He frowned.

Sonja chuckled. "You've never painted before, have you?"

He sent a good-natured scowl in her direction. "There's a first time for everything," he said quietly.

When Sonja's cheeks flamed and she looked away, he knew she'd gotten his message.

Louder, so Nellie might hear, he said, "To answer your first question, I think my secretary had something to do my being here."

"Heart has never participated. They—you," Nellie corrected, "didn't even reply to the letter we sent the year I was volunteer coordinator."

"Really?" Cole asked. "This is just the sort of community involvement that builds partnerships."

"That's right. A lot of companies, like the hospital, let people off to do this every year, and it's considered work time. Well, you're here now, so the letter got in the right hands this year," Nellie said.

They spent the next two hours painting the room before moving on to a smaller classroom. Easy conversation flowed about music and movies. Cole listened and laughed as Nellie and Sonja told stories about previous Volunteer Day moments. Through the morning, Cole remained cued into Sonja, tuned in to her laugh, her smile, those shorts, and those legs that kept him mighty distracted.

A maddening hint of arrogance surrounded him like an aura. Sonja found herself both attracted to and repelled by that part of him. Try as she might to deny it, each time she saw him, the pull got stronger and her defenses grew weaker.

From across the room she felt him watching her, assessing, waiting. He wanted her. And she wanted him.

Sonja's feelings for Cole had nothing to do with business or reason. Had she listened to reason she never would have set off on the course to destroy his company.

Had she listened to reason, she never would have found herself attracted to him. But reason had little, actually nothing, to do with the heat that raced through her at his touch.

Cole's body was powerfully lean. When he wrapped his arms around her, Sonja knew she'd feel enveloped, safe, secure. She wondered what it might be like to snake her own body up and down the hard length of his. Her mouth parted, and she slowly licked her lower lip.

Nellie ducked out to go in search of a rest room, and they were left unchaperoned for a moment.

"If you keep looking at me like that we're going to end up putting on a show that'll be the talk of these events for years to come."

Sonja was in the mood to play with fire. "How am I looking at you?"

"Like I'm the all-you-can-eat buffet at your favorite restaurant."

"Well, I do like buffets."

"Lunchtime, everybody!" The bullhorn sounded in their room for a moment, then moved on down the hall as the volunteer coordinator called everyone.

"Saved by the bell," Cole said. They put down their painting paraphernalia and headed to the gym.

The noonday meal consisted of boxed lunches catered and donated by a local deli and sandwich shop. The day being too beautiful to eat indoors, each volunteer grabbed a box and a can of soda or juice, then settled outside on the grass or at the curb to eat.

Sonja found a partially shady spot under an oak tree and settled her lunch in her lap.

"May I join you?" Cole asked.

"I was hoping you would."

Cole's lazy grin transformed his face. Sonja's breath caught. The harsh lines of stress usually found on his face were erased, transformed by the relaxing environment and—dare she hope?—her company.

He opened his white box and stared at the contents. "What do we have here?"

"Mine is turkey." Sonja leaned into him and peered at his lunch. Belatedly, she realized her breasts pressed into his arm. Her gaze shot up to his.

Cole's breathing deepened. "You've been making things very hard on me all morning."

Sonja's eyes went straight to his crotch, then back up his body. She watched him tense.

"Sonja?"

"Yes, Cole?" She wondered just what she might be agreeing to.

"Trade me your potato salad for my pasta salad."

Sonja released a pent up breath, then smiled. She plucked the small container from her box and handed it to him.

"Anything else?" she asked with more than a hint of mischievousness in her voice.

Cole's gaze took in her breasts, well concealed beneath the tunic and the tank top, but Sonja felt bare. She wondered if he could see the hardened buds that would-tell the story of where her thoughts remained.

"Eat," he commanded.

"That's what I had in mind," she murmured.

Cole's grunt could have meant anything, but then he glanced around to see who might be watching. No one.

All volunteers were busy polishing off their meals. Sonja and Cole ate in relative silence for a few moments.

"You said you like buffets, huh?"

Holding an apple, she nodded, then boldly asked, "What is this between us?"

"I think Rick James called it fire and desire."

Her mind told her to resist. They were, after all, in a very public place. But her body refused to listen to anything except the beat of her heart. The ache had to be assuaged. Now.

She placed a hand on his thigh. Cole leaned toward her to capture the kiss he'd wanted for so long.

"Oh, there you are, Mr. Heart."

The two jumped apart. Sonja's body thrummed in protest. She wanted to cry out her frustration. Instead, she folded her legs Indian style and took a bite of her apple.

Word had apparently gotten around about Cole's participation. In addition to the woman who hailed him, another two people headed their way, but before anyone could engage Cole in a conversation, the volunteer coordinator's bullhorn squawked with another announcement—this one about a group picture.

"We'd like to ask you something before you leave today," said the spokesman for the three.

Cole assured them he'd be happy to speak later, then watched as they hustled to the area where the photo would be taken.

"Where were we?" he asked.

"Still out in public," Sonja replied. She got up, tossed the remains of her lunch in a trash receptacle, and waited for Cole to rise.

When he did, she immediately noticed his problem, as would anyone else who bothered to look.

"This isn't over," he said.

"I didn't think it was."

A few minutes later, the volunteers crowded together for the group photo. Sonja wasn't at all surprised that Cole stood next to her.

"Okay, folks. Tighten up a bit," the photographer called out. "You there, tall guy in the gray sweatshirt, step behind and to your left a smidgen. You're blocking the shorter people."

Because it was to his advantage, Cole did as directed. They stood at the end of the group. Cole's left hand snaked around Sonja's waist, and he pulled her back to mold against his body.

"Okay. I almost have everybody. Get close now," the photographer directed.

Sonja's sharp intake of breath had nothing to do with the photo being shot and everything to do with the erection that pressed into her back and the teasing hand at her side.

She moaned.

"Come on now, Sonja," Nellie teased. "Taking a picture isn't that bad."

Sonja took a breath and sent a wavering smile toward Nellie. Cole increased the pressure as a finger stroked the tender area just below her breast. She swayed into him.

"Everybody say, 'Cheese!' "

All the volunteers grinned and yelled, "Cheese!"

Sonja's came out more like, "Ooohh."

Cole released her and stepped back as the group broke up. Sonja stood on the pavement willing her knees to support her. She turned toward Cole and caught her breath.

In his gray eyes burned the hot promise of raging

passion. She knew her own held need and desire. She couldn't tear her gaze away from his. She felt branded, marked, and she wanted to leave her own mark on him.

"Ready to hit the next rooms?" Nellie called.

Sonja and Cole continued to stare at each other. Sonja finally swallowed, prayed she had the strength to walk, and waved to Nellie. Without a word to Cole, she hastened back to her painting assignment.

The rest of the afternoon passed in agony for Sonja. The joy she should have gotten from the day had been replaced by unfulfilled need, by a sexual tension that left her taut as a bowstring.

Cole suffered, too. Each time Sonja bent to stir paint or stretched to reach a spot, his desire for her mounted. He'd been focused on business for so long that he'd forgotten what lust felt like. That was the only word to describe how hot she made him.

At the end of the day, a day that for Sonja and Cole seemed to last at least twelve hours, the volunteer coordinator thanked everyone, passed out T-shirts to each participant, then had them board the buses for downtown.

Cole slid in next to Sonja. They sat thigh to thigh, hers bare, his jean clad. Desire hummed between them, but neither spoke a word during the fifteen minute ride to city hall. After the volunteers unloaded and said their good-byes to each other, Cole turned to Sonja.

"Where's your car?" he asked.

"I left it in the garage and walked over here. It's just a couple of blocks. Where's yours?"

"Right over there," he said, pointing across the street to the volunteers' overflow parking area.

Cole's gaze dipped to her mouth. Then he looked into her eyes and read the answer he found there. "I

live in Williamsburg. It'll take thirty-five to forty minutes
to get to my house."

"I live fifteen minutes from here," she said.

Cole waited.

"You drive,' " she said. "I'll show you the way."

# Chapter 10

They barely got in the door before Cole turned her around, drew her close, and lowered his mouth to hers. This time, no interruption kept them from the thing they wanted most. Too impatient for the tentative exploration new lovers might savor, each sought the other with greedy impatience. Cole didn't have to force her lips open. Sonja willingly gave him the gift.

He ran quick hands over her bottom, roaming up under the frayed edges of her cutoffs. Her skin was smooth and soft, and everything he'd thought it might be. Lifting her to the erection that filled his jeans, Cole murmured something in her ear.

Sonja's answering chuckle was all woman, all promise.

As he roused her passion, his own grew stronger, bolder.

"Where's the bed?"

Sonja's eager hands ran along his neck, and she felt him tremble.

"Too far away," she murmured between the nibbles and nips she teased him with.

Cole bent and lifted her into his arms. Bold steps took them into a great room with large, inviting sofas displayed around a huge, brick fireplace. He stopped at the first one and lowered her to its cushioning comfort.

Clothes quickly disappeared, and in moments they were flesh to flesh.

"Beautiful," he murmured as he took in the whole of her.

"Exquisite," he said as his hand circled the plump breasts that had taunted him for weeks now. Between each word, each compliment, he planted kisses on her shoulders, her neck, her face, her earlobe.

Sonja moaned and ran her hand along the expanse of his back. Then she explored his dark brows and the small curls in his hair. She edged her finger along his lips and pressed a kiss there.

Not one to miss an opportunity, Cole expanded the kiss and coaxed more from her. Even while she kissed him, Sonja's hand lowered and then surrounded his erection. She squeezed, not gently, and a guttural growl came from the depth of him.

Cole crushed his lips across hers, and plunged the depths of her mouth.

Her reaction, swift and violently aroused, sent Cole over the edge. He thrust into her and heard her cry out in pain or in pleasure, he couldn't tell. Thinking he'd hurt her, Cole held still with a will he didn't know he possessed.

"Oh, Sonja. I'm sorry. I'm sorry. I just want you so—"

"Now!" she demanded as her body bucked and met him.

*WE INVITE YOU TO JOIN THE ONLY BOOK
CLUB THAT DELIVERS HEARTFELT ROMANCE
FEATURING AFRICAN AMERICAN HEROES AND
HEROINES IN STORIES THAT ARE RICH IN
PASSION AND CULTURAL SPICE...*

*And Your First 4 Books Are FREE!*

Arabesque is an exciting contemporary romance line offered by
BET Books, a division of BET Publications. Arabesque has been
so successful that our readers have asked us about direct home
delivery. Now you can start receiving four bestselling Arabesque
novels a month delivered right to your door. Subscribe now and
you'll get:

- ◇ 4 FREE Arabesque romances as our introductory gift—a value
  of almost $20! (pay only $1 to help cover postage &
  handling)
- ◇ 4 BRAND-NEW Arabesque romances
  delivered to your doorstep each month
  thereafter (usually arriving before
  they're available in bookstores!)
- ◇ 20% off each title—a savings of
  almost $4.00 each month
- ◇ FREE home delivery
- ◇ A FREE monthly newsletter,
  *Arabesque Romance News* that features
  author profiles, book previews and more
- ◇ No risks or obligations...in other words, you
  can cancel whenever you wish with no questions asked

So subscribe to Arabesque today and see why these books are
winning awards and readers' hearts.

After you've enjoyed our FREE gift of 4 Arabesque Romances,
you'll begin to receive monthly shipments of the newest
Arabesque titles. Each shipment will be yours to examine for 10
days. If you decide to keep the books, you'll pay the preferred
subscriber's price of just $4.00 per title. That's $16 for all 4
books with free home delivery. And if you want us to stop
sending books, just say the word.

*See why reviewers are raving about ARABESQUE
and order your FREE books today!*

# WE HAVE 4 FREE BOOKS FOR YOU!

ARABESQUE

(If the certificate is missing below, write to:
Zebra Home Subscription Service, Inc.,
120 Brighton Road, P.O. Box 5214, Clifton, New Jersey 07015-5214)

## FREE BOOK CERTIFICATE

*Yes!* Please send me 4 *Arabesque* Contemporary Romances without cost or obligation, billing me just $1 to help cover postage and handling. I understand that each month, I will be able to preview 4 brand-new *Arabesque* Contemporary Romances FREE for 10 days. Then, if I decide to keep them, I will pay the money-saving preferred subscriber's price of just $16.00 for all 4...that's a savings of almost $4 off the publisher's price with no additional charge for shipping and handling. I may return any shipment within 10 days and owe nothing, and I may cancel this subscription at any time. My 4 FREE books will be mine to keep in any case.

Name _____

Address _____ Apt. _____

City _____ State _____ Zip _____

Telephone ( ) _____

Signature _____ AR1298
(If under 18, parent, or guardian must sign.)

**ZEBRA HOME SUBSCRIPTION SERVICE, INC.**

120 BRIGHTON ROAD

P.O. BOX 5214

CLIFTON, NEW JERSEY 07015-5214

AFFIX
STAMP
HERE

"Oh," Cole cried.

With their hips locked and pleasure propelling them, Sonja and Cole reached for the fire and let it consume them.

Later, even while tiny tremors rippled though Sonja like aftershocks from an earthquake, they nestled on the wide sofa cushions, Cole's large body covering most of hers.

They remained quiet for a long time, the sound of their breathing the only noise between them.

"We went too fast," Cole said. "We skipped a few important things."

"Like a condom?" Sonja asked as she scooted up and a bit away from him.

*How could I have been so stupid?* She hadn't had a lot of sexual partners, just two to be exact, but she'd never, *ever* gotten so carried away that she forgot to take care of business.

Cole's steady gaze met hers. "That, too," he said.

For a tense moment, neither said anything as they processed the ramifications of that major oversight.

"I've had just two other lovers in my life, and I carry no diseases," Sonja eventually said. She knew that was probably an unusually low number, particularly for a woman of her age and sophistication, but Sonja had never taken sex lightly. Until now, she'd always been able to handle situations that got too heated too fast. With this man, all systems had shut down except the ones that sent her straight into his arms.

Cole remained quiet, so quiet that Sonja pushed at his chest.

"Cole?"

When he still didn't say anything, Sonja cursed and

pushed him with more force. "What have you given me?"

His eyes met hers and his large hand covered and caressed the smooth flat surface of her stomach.

"Maybe a baby," he said quietly.

Sonja looked horrified. "A baby! I don't think . . ." She stopped when she noticed the wonder and the longing in his eyes. The yearning she sensed in him gave her pause. She'd never even thought about children.

"Cole, it's not that time for me. Besides, we were talking about the other things people get when they don't use condoms."

"I'd never do anything to put you at risk or in danger. That includes anything we do here," he said, as the hand at her stomach stroked up toward her breasts and then down to the juncture of her thighs.

Her breath caught and she trembled. "Cole. . . . I . . . Um, hold that thought, please."

Forgetting once was an accident, forgetting twice was foolish. She kissed him, then twisted away and then up. "I'll be right back."

She knew he watched as she disappeared. True to her word, she came right back with a handful of condoms. Cole's eyebrows rose at the number.

She smiled and shrugged. "Just in case."

"Come here."

Sonja leaned forward. Their kiss was light and sweet. He circled a hand around her waist and pulled her to him, caressing, soothing, preparing her. They made erotic play of putting the sheaf on Cole, then he stroked her. A tremor inside Sonja heated her thighs and groin, her hips arched into his caress.

Cole looked into her eyes and smiled as he watched them drift shut. His mouth traced the trail his hand had taken. With licks and kisses he roamed up one side of her lithe body, pausing to feast at the full display her breasts presented. Her soft mewling pleas for more gave Cole an intense satisfaction. With maddeningly measured moves, he meandered his way, slowly, slowly, down the other side of her body, giving every inch of her the proper respect and attention due a goddess.

Sonja abandoned herself to the whirl of sensation that whipped and twirled through her. It was too much, not enough, just right. She cried out. She reached for him, but he ignored her.

Cole's indulgent chuckle promised more. Sonja wasn't sure if she could stand it.

He lifted away from her, then shifted her body to the center of the sofa. Positioning himself between her legs, he leaned over her and blew a gentle breath up and across her abdomen.

She shivered and moaned what sounded like, "Please, no more."

"Want me to stop?" he murmured.

"No. More," she breathed, the single syllable words all she could manage.

Sonja's need was taut, hot, and intense, so close she wanted to cry out her frustration. Instead, she lifted hips to him, and Cole's head bent to her in a raw act of possession. Sonja yielded to him, completely surrendered, and soared to a pleasure she hadn't known was possible.

Later, drained, she lay sated beneath him.

Cole was damn pleased with himself, and smiled his contentment.

"You don't have to look so cocky," she said when she could finally speak.

"Why shouldn't I? Look at you."

Sonja met his gaze, then let it travel along as much of the length of him she could see. He was hard, all man. And hers.

"I'd rather look at you," she said. Cole's erection seemed to grow larger as it pressed against her leg. She stroked him and got pleasure from his quick intake of breath followed by a deep moan.

"Two can play your game," she said.

"Show me more."

Sonja slipped off the sofa and stood before him in naked glory. He reached for her, ready to take her on the floor. But Sonja clasped his hand and led him to her bedroom.

There, they played hard and fast, then easy and slow. They explored each other and whispered the words lovers share. Eventually they slept in a tangle of legs and sheets.

Much later, Sonja awoke to a growling stomach. Without disturbing Cole she found a light robe, wrapped it about her body, and made her way to her kitchen. There she prepared a light breakfast of omelets and fresh fruit.

She carried their meal on a tray to her bedroom. As she passed through the door, Cole reached for her in his sleep. The empty place stirred him. Instantly awake he sat up and looked around.

"Sustenance," Sonja said as she approached and settled the tray on the bed.

"I need a different kind of sustenance," Cole said.

"Maybe I should call you Superman," Sonja said as she plucked a piece of melon from the edge of the plate. She leaned forward, offering it to Cole. But his attention remain locked on the fullness of her breasts, a far more tempting fruit he had a clear view of through her gaping robe.

"I'm hungry," Sonja said. "More of that after this."

"Well, let's hurry up and eat."

# Chapter 11

Sweet kisses along her jaw, her neck, and shoulder woke Sonja several hours before dawn. Snuggling her backside into Cole's embrace, she smiled lazily.

"Good morning," Cole murmured.

"Mmm." She sighed. "What time is it?"

"A little after four. I need to leave."

Sonja turned, and Cole sat up on an elbow supported by plump pillows.

She stared into his eyes. "What does this mean?"

Cole ran his hand along her hairline and then the strands of hair that went in several directions at her temple.

Sonja forgot about her question and ran a quick hand through her hair, hoping to give a little shape to her sleep and sex-tossed tresses. "I forgot to sleep pretty."

His indulgent smile warmed her.

"What's sleeping pretty?"

Sonja smiled. "It's a female thing."

His hand meandered to her breast and the nipple that puckered and hardened at his touch. "A female thing like this?" he asked.

Sonja moaned and her back arched. Cole welcomed the invitation. He shed the sheet tangled between their legs and lowered his body onto hers. And they loved again. This time slowly.

Too soon, Cole glanced at the clock by her bedside. He spread kisses along her jaw and then got up.

"Sorry to kiss and leave, but I need to get to work."

Sonja's eyes widened. She stared at his bare behind as he pulled on his briefs.

It hit her, then.

*Oh, my God. What have I done?*

The reminder about his job had the effect of ice water down her back. Trembling hands covered her mouth as she watched him dress. She'd slept with Cole Heart, a man she'd sworn to hate. Cole Heart, her enemy and the symbolic head of her persecution. How could she have compromised herself this way?

Cole finished dressing, and Sonja sat in the middle of her bed looking devastated.

With his Community Volunteer Day hat in hand, he turned to her. "I'll call you later."

The ramifications of her actions rolled through Sonja, leaving her breathless, shell-shocked. Unable to speak, she simply nodded. Suddenly self-conscious, she yanked the sheet from the foot of the bed and wrapped it toga style about her body as she slid from bed to let him out of the house.

At her front door, Cole paused. "We left your car downtown.

"I have another one in the garage," she answered mindlessly. Sonja's thoughts were occupied by how she'd let the physical demands of her body override the good sense of her head.

Cole chuckled. "So do I. Cars are my only vice."

She sent a vague smile his way, then reached around him to open the door. The faster he got out of her house, the sooner she could get herself together.

Cole's hand cupped her face. "I'm glad this happened," he said. "You've made me realize that there are things more important, and more enjoyable, than working."

He pressed his lips to hers in what should have been a tender farewell kiss. But Sonja's eyes remained open the entire time. He said good-bye, then waved as he headed around the cobbled walkway to his car.

Sonja shut the door and leaned against it with a heavy sigh. Her gaze took in the elegant foyer of her home, but she didn't see any of it. She wiped a hand across her mouth, then stared at her hand and at the sheet that covered her naked body.

"What have I done?"

The regret stayed with her throughout the day. She'd arrived at work later than intended, and then had another fight with Brian after the staff meeting.

"I can take my talent elsewhere, you know," he threatened. "You're not the only game in town."

Now Sonja sat in her chair staring out at the view. Usually the river view and the traffic settled her, made her feel as if she were the only constant in a fast-paced, always moving world. But today she felt like a castaway stranded on a desert island.

She went through the motions for another few hours before just calling the entire day a waste.

"I'm leaving," she told her secretary. "Page me if something comes up."

"Sonja, are you okay?"

She smiled at the concern in her employee's voice. "No, but I will be."

Sonja went to her spa and headed to the rowing machines. The repetitive motions always soothed her while allowing her to think. Working her body freed her mind to evaluate and consider options, to sort the wheat from the chaff. She did some of her best creative work while rowing.

By the time she'd finished her total workout she still couldn't claim to be in better spirits. Coming to grips with what she'd done wasn't the hard part. She'd achieved clarity, but it came at the high price of resolution. What she'd resolved added yet another layer to the problem. The difficulty lay in the fact that she wanted to sleep with him again.

Everyone around Cole noticed the change in him. He smiled and whistled and complimented people. He seemed relaxed, easy. Not once during the day did he reach for his bottle of antacid.

"Did you make a bundle on the stock market or something?" Lance asked.

Cole laughed, and Lance looked at his uncle as if he'd been replaced by an identical twin alien.

"No. Why do you say that?"

Lance warily eyed Cole as the two walked through their Hampton store. "Well, with most people, money or sex will put them in a good mood. You just told me it isn't money. I've never seen you like this."

"Like what?"

"Happy. Relaxed. Like you just got laid, and it was *good,*" he added.

Cole's amused grin stopped Lance cold. A woman with a stroller rolled right into him. Lance apologized profusely, picked up the sleeping baby's bottle, and handed it to her. The woman steered around them, and still Lance stood there.

"Come on," Cole prodded. "I have something I need to pick up. You're holding up the works."

Lance hurried to catch up. "Are you telling me you had sex? *You* slept with somebody?' "

"Must you make a public announcement?"

Lance was having trouble with this. "When did you have time to sleep with somebody? When did you have time to *meet* anybody?"

Cole slapped him on the back and winked. "You make time for the important things." Then, whistling, Cole made his way to the gift department.

Lance stood in the middle of the floor with his mouth hanging open.

Even his mother's telephone call that evening didn't squelch Cole's good mood.

"I hear you were Mr. Congeniality today."

"For someone who's seldom at the enclave, you sure know a lot about what happens every day."

"I don't want to fight, Coleman."

"Neither do I, Mother. What can I do for you?"

"I was just calling to chat," she said. "Would you like to have dinner with me Thursday night?"

"Let me check my book in the morning. Mason scheduled a night meeting this week. I forgot to check the day and time before I left."

There was silence on the other end of the line.

"Mom?"

Virginia raised an elegant eyebrow and looked at the telephone. Cole rarely, if ever, called her Mom. He *never* left his daybook planner at work, and he usually could spout his schedule for the next month. Was that indeed her son on the line?

Lance had given her an earful about Cole's odd behavior. Concerned but not quite sure how to broach the topic, Virginia let it go for now.

Lance might have been the only person to directly question Cole's good mood, but he wasn't the only person who'd come to the same conclusion about the source. Her grandson's comment about Cole having a date, coupled with Virginia's intelligence inside the enclave duly reporting the rumors swirling about Heart Federated's CEO, had her wondering.

She finished the conversation, then replaced the receiver with trembling hands. Cole had never shown a tendency to follow in his father's philandering footsteps. And now was not the time to start, particularly with Sonja Pride. That Pride woman was the only female Cole seemed to express any interest in lately.

"Oh, Lord. We could have a problem."

Then she cursed her dead husband.

Virginia's relationship with Coleman II had always been clear. He knew where home was, and he kept her in diamonds and furs. She didn't like his sleeping around one bit, but knew when to keep her mouth shut. Not very many people knew all the secrets about the Heart family. But Virginia knew them, and so did her brother-in-law, Jimmy.

She bit her lip and reached for the telephone. Jimmy had his faults, but he might have some advice on how to deal with this situation. She replaced the receiver after punching the first two numbers.

"Stay calm, Virginia," she coached herself. "Crisis is

your middle name, but this might not be a crisis. It could be anybody.''

Justine claimed no prior knowledge about Sonja Pride, but Virginia knew her sister-in-law like the back of her hand. Justine had deliberately and viciously poked her finger in a long dormant hornets' nest. The Heart past was a tangle of lies, half-truths, and cover-ups. And Jussie had contributed more than her share, a fact she thought no one knew.

"Folks in glass houses shouldn't run around throwing stones," Virginia said.

Justine had some nerve jeopardizing Cole and the financial stability of the company. Virginia didn't care a whit about Heart Federated, but she'd grown mighty accustomed to her life style, one that had been financed by the stores for a long time.

Virginia smiled. She had the perfect foil for Justine, as well as a first-rate snoop detective, right at her finger-tips. She reached for the telephone to call her niece Mallory. Mallory doted on her, and with the right incentive, could be persuaded to do a little digging.

The first and most important thing Virginia had to determine was who her son was sleeping with. At her large waterfront home in Hampton, Virginia Heart paced the floor, hoping against hope.

When Sonja fell into bed that night, her nerves were back in a tangled mess. For the first time since she'd determined her goal and set herself on a clear course, she had doubts . . . the kind inspired by guilt.

Sleepless nights had never haunted her. Until now.

* * *

Cole lay in his bed thinking about the incredible woman he'd spent the previous day and night with. He didn't have her home telephone number, and had to no avail harassed a directory assistance operator about the emergency nature of the call he needed to make, if only she'd give up the number. He cherished his own privacy and understood the need for unlisted phone numbers, but this was different.

With the directions indelibly stamped in his memory, twice now he'd gotten up to go to her house. On each occasion he'd vetoed the move. He didn't want to crowd Sonja, and he didn't want her to think he had a one-track mind.

But, of course, he did. Cole folded his arms under his head and stared at the ceiling. Now that he'd gotten a taste, he wanted more . . . and more . . . and more.

Lance was right. Cole didn't have time for sex, or for the dates and the games that usually went along with getting any. So, focusing on what really mattered, he'd abstained. He also had no intention of being a world-class skirt chaser like his father. Had Coleman Heart paid more attention to business, the company wouldn't be in its current vulnerable state.

Of course, Cole had to concede, if intercourse with any woman before Sonja had been as good as what they shared, he probably wouldn't have sworn off it so easily. But now . . .

Just the thought of Sonja's cool hands on his hot flesh aroused him. Cole cursed, rolled over, and punched a pillow. It was going to be a long, lonely night.

# Chapter 12

Early the next morning Mason placed a bottle of antacid on Cole's desk along with a folder of correspondence and three diskettes. He mumbled "Thanks," without taking his eyes off his computer monitor.

"Mr. Heart, there's something you need to know."

"What is it?"

"It's important."

Cole glanced at Mason, who stood at the edge of his desk. She'd been with him nine years now, first as his part-time assistant, then later as secretary, and now executive assistant. Unlike some of his flesh and blood she was completely loyal. She knew the value of his work, and how much time it took. If she said something was important, it was.

"What?" That came out more gruff than intended or warranted. Lucky for him, Mason understood his shorthand speech.

"Miss Heart—Mallory—" she clarified before he

asked which one, "has been asking a lot of not quite subtle questions."

Cole sat back in his chair. "My cousin is a lot of things, subtle not being one of them. What kind of questions, and to whom?"

"Well, she's asked a couple of secretaries if they've noticed a change in you, if they thought you were preoccupied with something or someone else," she said, stressing the *someone* part.

"And?" Cole prompted.

Mason looked away, then met his gaze head on. "You've been the topic of more than one conversation in the last few weeks."

He chuckled. "It's good to keep folks on their toes. Anything else?"

"She asked me if you'd sent flowers, candy, or mementos to anyone recently."

Cole frowned and his lips thinned. "And you said?"

Mason stood erect. "I told her I didn't know anything about your personal affairs."

Cole grinned. "Excellent. Did you get that crystal paperweight mailed out?"

She nodded, smiling back. "Ms. Pride should get it in this afternoon's mail."

"What do you think Mallory's up to?" he asked.

"Her usual," Mason said dryly. Then color flooded her cheeks as she realized what she'd said. "I'm sorry, I didn't mean—"

Cole's chuckle eased her. "You know the real deal. Don't try to sugarcoat it or pretend otherwise."

"If I may speak frankly?" she asked. When Cole nodded, she continued. "I don't know everything about your relationship with Mallory and Mrs. Heart—Justine. But I do know that I'd be careful, very careful, around them. That last board meeting was the tip of the ice-berg.''

Cole knew that, but wondered what additional intelligence Mason might have come across. "In what way?"

With both hands on his desk, Mason leaned forward. "I've heard some talk, not completely confirmed of course, that Mallory, your aunt, and someone else from the family had a hush-hush meeting with Knight and Kraus. The meeting was two weeks *after* the board voted to reject their proposal."

Dammit all!

"Can your sources find out what happened?"

"I can try, but it's not likely. That was on the Q-T from someone reliable who overheard speculation on the meeting."

*"Thanks,* Mason," Cole said.

Forewarned was forearmed where his relatives were concerned. Early on he'd learned that he had to watch his back if he wanted to survive. The scowl deepened on his face as he turned over the possibilities of what that secret meeting might have been about. He could be sure of just one thing: If Mallory and his aunt were scurrying around on the sly, it was with the sole purpose of making him look bad.

"Did you take your blood pressure medicine, Mr. Heart?"

"Yes, Mother," he said, his tone telling her he wasn't upset with her intelligence gathering.

Mason smiled, nodded, then headed to her office. Cole turned back to his monitor.

*Mallory,* he thought, *you would have been a perfect Medici. What drama are you orchestrating now?*

\* \* \*

He found out two hours later when he took a call from a panicked general manager who'd spotted a Knight and Kraus scout team in the Virginia Beach store. Cole encouraged the store managers to keep in touch with him, but most preferred to work directly with their division heads.

"Marty, how do you know they were from K&K?" Cole asked.

"I met one of them, a buyer, at a trade show last year. She's not the type you forget easily."

"Well, what did they want?"

"She said she was in town and needed a scarf."

Cole reached for his antacid and tried to keep the impatience out of his voice. "You called me because a woman wanted to buy a scarf?"

"Given what you said the other day and the mystery shoppers being in the stores, I assumed you'd want to know."

"Okay. Anything else?"

"They looked like they were doing more than shopping. One was taking notes. All three of them were trying not to be conspicuous in a conspicuous sort of way."

Cole nodded. After his own experience as a mystery shopper, he knew what that was like.

And he knew time was running out.

After talking to the store manager Cole spent the rest of the day and evening lobbying some of his relatives. The fence straddlers would be important to have as allies when the time came. He lunched with an aunt, took chocolates to another, and had dinner with a distant, shareholding cousin. They all seemed to understand his point, and the importance of solidarity.

He could only hope his effort was enough.

\* \* \*

Sonja stared at the proposal on her desk. This simple request from a mid-western department store chain had launched her entire plan to propel the downfall of Heart Federated. She'd viewed the proposal from Claiborne Bros. as the perfect opportunity to get into Heart, to assess its weaknesses and then legally and ethically hand the findings over to the larger chain that was considering moving to the area.

If Claiborne Bros. moved into the market, it would spell the end of the Heart stores. In the beginning, that's what she'd wanted more than anything in the world. She wanted to see the Hearts bowed, if not outright broken. The Claiborne people had given her the perfect means to meet her goal—and The Pride Group would even make money on the deal.

Out of nowhere she'd gotten the call about Heart wanting a quick and dirty assessment of its customer service practices. At the time it had seemed like providence telling her she was justified in her plans, that the universal law of "what goes around, comes around" was about to be proven with the Heart family.

But now that she'd gotten to know Cole Heart a little better—more importantly, now that she'd slept with the man—she was having a change of heart.

Could she still go through with her plan to sell him out this way? Of course she could, part of her urged.

Claiborne could get data from another market research firm, but Sonja's company didn't have the reputation of being the best for nothing. No outfit could deliver like The Pride Group. It was a fact that usually brought Sonja a measure of comfort in a field where complacency was the death knell.

Sonja rubbed her eyes. If the Claiborne Bros. contract eventually extended to all their retail and subsidiary outfits, the potential existed to increase The Pride Group's revenue by almost a fourth. That wasn't a figure to ignore—even with the money the new Robinson account would bring.

She pushed the envelope from time to time, but she'd never done an outright unethical or dishonest thing in her life. Payback remained a strong motivater, but if she just talked to Cole about her past experiences in his stores and with his family, maybe that would be enough to eliminate the bloodlust she sometimes felt toward the Hearts.

She'd put the Claiborne people off for more than a month now, and knew if she did any longer they would take their business to a rival research group.

She turned to her PC and did a fast calculation on how much money she'd lose if she wimped out. Even as she stared at the number, a pretty big one, her heart wasn't in it.

"Not the way it was, at least."

Money didn't turn her on. She'd already made more than she'd ever thought she might. Her mother would never know another day of poverty. Sonja sat there letting the consequences of each possible path roll through her head.

Her line rang, and her secretary announced Cole Heart.

Sonja's palms broke out in a sweat. She licked her lips, even fluffed her hair, before picking up the receiver.

"Hello, Cole."

"Hi."

His voice was low, intimate. Sonja's body responded

to the husky tone even as her mind raced a mile a minute, still weighing options and scenarios.

"I've been thinking about you," he said.

A soft knock at Sonja's open door made her look up from the sudden and intense study of her fingernails. Sonja's secretary tipped in, placed a package on her desk, then tiptoed out, closing the door behind her.

She lifted the top and removed tissue paper and velvet lining.

Hoping for a neutral tone, she said, "I hope you enjoyed Volunteer Day yesterday."

If she kept her hands occupied, maybe her mind wouldn't stray down unwanted paths. Sonja upended the box, and a crystal paperweight fell into her waiting hand. The piece was gorgeous in its simplicity. On each side a word was etched: Truth. Integrity. Spirit. Dedication. She searched for a card, but none seemed to be included with the package.

"Oh, I did. Very much," he said. "So much so that I was hoping there might be another opportunity to, uh, volunteer sometime really soon."

The heavy piece fell to her desk with a dull thud. "I, uh . . ."

Cole's chuckle in her ear didn't help matters. "I understand you can't talk right now."

"That's not it. There's something I need to tell you."

"Excellent. Tell me over dinner tonight."

Dinner was not at all what she had in mind, but she couldn't very well tell him over the telephone that she'd planned to sabotage his company's future, could she? Sonja thought about it for a moment. Actually, she *could* be ruthless when she chose.

"Sonja, are you still there?"

"Yes."

"Dinner tonight. I promise to behave like a gentleman."

"I don't know, Cole. I have some work to do."

"You have to eat. And I can tell you about the meeting I had with my general managers regarding your research and findings to date."

She stared down at the paperweight: Truth. Integrity. Spirit. Dedication. *Confess,* her conscience nudged. "Cole, I—"

He cut her off. "Tell me at dinner. I have an incoming call I need to take. Eight o'clock at The Trellis in Williamsburg."

His bossiness grated. Sonja's hackles rose, and she sat up in her chair. Cole assumed a lot, and did a lot of demanding. The man was pushy, arrogant, and rude.

"Cole?"

A dial tone answered back. Sonja put the phone down. It took her a few moments to get her nerves together and then calm down. Cole Heart deserved whatever he got. She planned to give him a piece of her mind tonight.

The Trellis was one of the busiest and most popular restaurants in the Williamsburg historic area. Tourists and locals alike enjoyed the food, the atmosphere, and the world-class desserts. It wasn't the sort of place to have a hissy fit.

By the time eight arrived the only thing on Sonja's mind was getting something to eat. She hadn't eaten since noon, and was starving. Cole arrived before her, and greeted her as she came up the walkway.

Sonja held her hand out for a shake, but he bent to her and kissed her on the cheek. "Hello."

Cole Heart had his faults, but the man could make a suit talk. The double-breasted, ultramarine suit made him appear taller and even more commanding—and demanding—than she'd ever seen him.

Of course, the fact that she knew what he looked like under that suit contributed to Sonja's weak knees. A woman of strength, she made her back sturdy even as her face flamed.

"Hello," she answered. Then she wondered irrationally if everyone in the restaurant terrace area knew they'd slept together.

Determined to make this nothing more than a business dinner, she'd refused to go home and change clothes. Mr. Perfection probably looked as crisp as he had at 4 P.M., after almost a full day's work. After her own long day, Sonja figured her teal flounce suit was ready for the dry cleaner.

"Our table is ready."

Taking in the line of people waiting, Sonja realized again the clout the Hearts wielded. Of course he had clout. He hailed from one of the most widely known families in the area.

With a hand at her waist Cole guided Sonja, who followed the hostess to their table, one of the best in the house. Cole seated Sonja, then slipped out of his suit jacket. She found something incredibly sexy about the outline of his white T-shirt through his dress shirt.

Sonja let out an unsteady breath as she watched him take his seat. Elegant sapphire cufflinks complemented his suit, and the bold tie with its wild reds, yellows, and blues reminded her he was a man who paid attention to detail. She knew that from the thoroughly meticulous way he'd roamed her body, too.

By removing his jacket Cole set the relaxed tone of

the evening. As the candle at their table flickered, Cole told her about his hopes and dreams for Heart. Sonja felt a flicker of remorse, but let it pass. There was too much she found fascinating about this man to spoil the night with talk of confessions and regrets. There would be time later, not now when they were mellow and enjoying each other's company. *Like real people,* she thought.

Through their meals and a rich chocolate dessert which they shared, Sonja laughed and good-naturedly one-upped him on stories about travels. Even though their opinions on books and music ran opposite, they found they both had tropical fish, and enjoyed the same types of movies.

"I suppose you're one of those women who saw *Titanic* about eighty times," Cole said.

"Actually, no. My speed is more along the lines of *Air Force One* and the last Bond film."

"And I take it you rooted for the feminist fighter?"

Sonja smiled. "That's right. But she did get her man in the end."

Her provocative words seemed to ignite a sensuous flame in Cole's eyes. "Yes, she did, didn't she?" A huskiness she hadn't noticed before crept into his voice.

He studied her face for an extra beat, long enough for Sonja's heart rate to slow and then beat double-time.

Sonja licked suddenly dry lips and reached for her wineglass. It was empty. Cole poured her more from the bottle they shared.

"You make me forget propriety, Ms. Pride."

She sipped from her glass. "Propriety is a good thing."

His smile, as intimate as a kiss, made Sonja's insides

melt. "Sometimes," he said. "At other times, as in a crowded restaurant, it's just a downright nuisance."

Sonja had the sudden urge to fan herself, but didn't want Cole to know how his words affected her.

Cole leaned forward and reached across the table for her hand.

"What we had yesterday was spectacular."

"It shouldn't have happened," Sonja said.

"It was meant to happen," Cole countered. "All my life I've waited for someone who could make me lose my head. I was beginning to think it would never happen. I was pretty much resigned to the fact that incomparable women didn't exist. Then you walked into my life."

"We have a business relationship," Sonja insisted.

He leaned even closer. "And do you sleep with all your clients?"

"How dare—"

He cut her off. "I didn't think so. I think what we have is pretty special."

"We don't have anything. You don't know me."

"I know what matters."

Sonja could have argued with him, but she wasn't in the mood. Her body cried out for his touch, even while her head told her to get out of the deep water. Problem was, she didn't like that sensible message, not one bit.

At her car a little while later, Cole tried to convince her to swing by his house to see his wall aquarium. It was on her way home, he insisted. Sonja was intrigued, but also savvy enough to know that in spite of his words the invitation still amounted to the old makeout invitation: "Let me show you my etchings."

She tried to give him a little wave and then duck into her Lexus, but Cole stopped her with one arm around her waist.

"Thank you," he said.

"For what?"

Cole stared at her face so long that Sonja wondered if she'd suddenly developed a pimple or wart.

"For being beautiful and challenging, and smart and forthright. I like all of those things about you."

Everything was fine until he got to the forthright part. A stab of guilt pricked her.

"Cole, there's something—"

He silenced her with a finger at her lips. A moment later, his lips replaced that finger. All thought, rational and otherwise, fled from Sonja's head. Her arms drifted up his chest and then around his neck. Giving herself to the passion of the kiss came easily, so easily that Sonja briefly reconsidered his invitation to go home with him.

With one final kiss, Cole stepped away and opened her car door. Without a word and while she still had control of her actions, Sonja slipped in and pulled on her seatbelt.

It wasn't until Sonja was driving home that it dawned on her: They hadn't talked business at all. Cole Heart had finagled a date and she'd fallen hook, line, and sinker.

# Chapter 13

The investigation wasn't going at all according to Virginia's plans. Here it was two weeks later, and she knew precious little else about her son's lover than when Lance first told her he was seeing someone. Had Cole been any other man, Virginia might have entertained the notion that nothing was going on in his life. But the blood of cheating Hearts ran through her son's veins. From firsthand, painful experience, Virginia knew just how indiscreet some Heart men could be when they so chose.

After her first feeble attempts at sleuthing, Mallory had been totally unresponsive to Virginia's manipulation, and was off doing whatever it was that she did. According to Cole, Mallory's chief purpose in life was to torment him.

"Those two never got along," she told her brother-in-law Jimmy.

"You haven't listened to a word I've been saying, Ginny."

"Don't call me that. You know I abhor nicknames."

Jimmy blew cigar smoke in her direction.

Virginia waved a hand in the air to clear it. "Disgusting habit, you know."

"Yep."

Virginia sighed. "James, what are we going to do?"

"We? I suggest you go shopping or something. I'm going to get myself a good seat. This meeting next week promises to be a good one." Jimmy chuckled. "Think we ought to have an ambulance standing by in case Cole and Mallory go at it one-on-one?"

"I fail to see the humor. I'm here trying to divert a crisis."

"No, you're not. You're meddling as usual. Cole is a grown man. He ought to be able to get himself a little piece without his mama all in the mix."

"You are so crude."

Jimmy grinned. For a moment, Virginia was reminded of her husband. She found herself torn between twin desires to slap him and kiss him. The moment passed, thank goodness.

"But what if it's—" Virginia couldn't even bring herself to say the words.

"Chances are slim to none. You know that. Cole with a woman? Please. I think the boy is a virgin."

Virginia's long-suffering sigh filled the parlor at her house. James truly tried her patience sometimes.

"Don't sigh, Ginny girl. I know you're still trying to get over the fact you married the wrong brother. I'm available now to ease your grief."

Virginia's glare just made him chuckle. "Don't let the door hit you on your way out, James."

In her usual flurry of silk, Virginia swept from the room. Jimmy laughed out loud. He hoped Mallory got half as much joy out of tormenting Cole as he got out of harassing the snooty Virginia.

Ginny's fretting usually had a granule of truth, so Jimmy thought he'd call on his sister-in-law next. Justine thrived on instigating trouble. What his brother had ever seen in her Jimmy still hadn't figured out, even after forty odd years. But John had wanted her, so Jimmy'd made it happen.

Today, he found her at the country club sipping a club soda. Jimmy ordered scotch, then joined his sister-in-law on the veranda.

"What trouble are you brewing?" he asked.

"Can't you ever just say 'hello'?"

"Nope. How much support do you think he has?"

"Who?"

Jimmy cocked his head and pursed his lips. "Jussie, act like a grownup for a change."

Justine pouted. "I don't know. According to my sources, he's been making the rounds for the last two weeks. To what avail, I don't know."

"Bet you don't know nothing about a secret meeting over to Knight and Kraus either, huh?"

She cut her eyes at him. "Don't you have anything better to do with your time?"

He kicked his feet up on a low table. "Spending time with my favorite sister-in-law is what I enjoy most."

Justine's derisive snort let him know what she thought of that. Jimmy just chuckled.

"Whose side are you on, anyway?" she demanded.

"The side that has my butt covered."

"That's a mighty big territory."

Jimmy scratched his fingers in the air. "Meow."

Justine smiled.

For a moment, they sipped their drinks in solitude.

"The young ones deserve a chance to show what they can do," Jimmy said.

"That's right. And had Mallory been given her rightful shot at the chairmanship, we wouldn't be in this mess now."

"Um hmm. And I suppose those checks we send to keep the peace on your branch of the family tree are just chump change. Nothing to do with all that red ink, huh?"

Justine darted frantic eyes to her right and left. "Hush."

"What? Afraid somebody might find out about your little secret?"

"Dammit, Jimmy."

"I'm just saying the pot shouldn't be calling the kettle black."

"We should sell," Justine said adamantly. "I'm sick of this."

"You really don't have much say in the matter. Or have you forgotten that fact?" He rubbed his chin reflectively, then smirked at her. "But, of course, you haven't forgotten. That's why you make so much fuss. It's the only thing you *can* do."

Jimmy chuckled at his little joke. Justine cut cold eyes at him.

"Mallory knows what's best for herself, for the company *and* for her mother. With the money we'll earn from dumping those dinosaurs, she'll be able to write her own ticket."

Jimmy got up, washed down the rest of his drink and placed the glass on the small table. "Maybe before you dump the dinosaurs, you ought to tell the *rightful* heir that his legacy is being thrown away.''

They stared at each other for tense moments. Then tears brimmed in Justine's eyes. "I hate you, Jimmy Heart. I hate you.''

"Yeah, so what else is new?''

Justine threw her glass at him, but Jimmy anticipated the move and ducked aside. Glass and ice crashed to the veranda floor. Jimmy brushed a few drops of soda from his sports jacket and chuckled as he turned his back on his sister-in-law.

With that seed planted, it was time for him to pay a call on Cole.


Jimmy went to the enclave, where he still maintained an office. His elaborately decorated suite suited him just fine when he felt like coming to work.

"Oh, good afternoon, Mr. Heart. We weren't expecting you today. Would you like me to call your secretary for you?''

He waved away the receptionist at the entry of the enclave. "Nah, don't bother her. She usually leaves a pile on the desk if there's something I need. Cole in?''

The woman nodded. Jimmy winked at her and made his way around the circular hall. He paused in his office long enough to get himself a drink. Then he went in search of Cole.

"Hey, Mason.''

She looked up from her dictation. "Hello, Mr. Heart. How are you today?''

"Just fine. Where's Cole?''

"He's in a meeting until three.''

"Tell him I need to talk to him," Jimmy said.

"He's with some people now, Mr. Heart."

Jimmy sipped from his drink, then placed the glass on Mason's desk. "Company business?"

"Yes, of course."

Jimmy thumped his chest and strode toward Cole's closed door. "I'm the company."

Mason barely had time to buzz Cole an alert before Jimmy boldly let himself in.

The office was empty. Jimmy headed to the small conference room adjacent to the office. There Cole, Lance, Sonja Pride, a guy Jimmy didn't know, and two store general managers huddled around a flip chart. The woman was a beauty. Her auburn hair and lush figure reminded Jimmy of his wife when she'd cared a damn about her looks.

"I'm sorry, Mr. Heart," Mason said from around Jimmy.

Lance and the store managers turned and said hello.

"It's okay, Mason. Uncle Jimmy, what can I do for you? We're in the middle of something."

"I need to talk to you. It's important."

Cole introduced Jimmy to Sonja and to the other man, then nodded toward The Pride Group representatives.

"Brian, Sonja, continue. I'll be right back."

The two men walked into Cole's office and shut the door.

"Good guard dog you have out there, Cole," Jimmy said indicating Mason's office. "And that's a nice piece in there, too," he said nodding toward the conference room.

"We might be privately owned and operated, Uncle Jimmy, but the sexual harassment laws still apply."

Jimmy rolled his eyes. "Men are still men, and women are still women."

Cole sat on the edge of his desk. "You said you had something to tell me."

Jimmy roamed over to the wet bar in Cole's office. He muttered when he didn't see any scotch. "Your daddy used to keep this place well stocked. I don't see anything but juice, bottled water, and soda pop."

"I'm not my father, a fact I have to keep reminding everyone of around here."

"You sure are touchy about that."

"Wouldn't you be? My father—your brother—died in here screwing his girlfriend on his desk."

Jimmy took a look at Cole's impressive hardwood desk. "Yeah, and that's the first thing you got out of here, too."

"Uncle Jimmy, I saw you because you don't generally barge into my office. I'm sure you didn't come here to tell me about the ancient history of my father and his affairs."

Jimmy walked around. One boring watercolor was on the wall opposite Cole's desk. A couple of plants broke some of the monotony. Jimmy decided the office had zilch personality, sort of like Cole. When nothing of interest caught his attention, he turned back to his nephew.

"I know you think your Daddy and I ran this company into the ground, but we did what we had to do to make it. There were circumstances we had to deal with. You'll understand that sometime before you die."

Cole folded his arms, waiting for Jimmy to get to the point.

"You do that just like Pops. He used to sit at the edge of his desk and scowl at me, Coleman, and Johnny. Told us all we had to fly right or he wasn't leaving us a dime in his will.''

"So you decided to spend all the money when you got your hands on it? I've been reviewing the financials, Uncle Jimmy. There are a whole lot of expenditures that seem redundant, unnecessary, and downright questionable.''

"We got audited when we were supposed to, and everything always checked out.''

"Of course, everything checked out. As chief financial officer, it was your job to make sure everything seemed on the up and up.''

"What are you implying?''

"Nothing you don't already know,'' Cole said.

Jimmy smiled. "That's why I've always liked you. You've got a good head on your shoulders. Not afraid to speak your mind.''

Cole got up and went behind his desk to take a seat. It was Jimmy's turn to stand at the edge of the desk. He reached for a brass figurine of three little monkeys.

"Lord, where'd you find this?'' Jimmy said. "I haven't seen that in years.''

"Pops gave it to me when I graduated from college. Seeing no evil, hearing no evil, and speaking no evil is a good way get yourself in trouble.''

"Depends on your perspective,'' Jimmy muttered.

"I have people waiting for me,'' Cole reminded.

Jimmy put the figurine down and looked Cole in the eye. "I'm worried about next week.''

That got Cole's attention. "Why?''

"Despite what you might believe, I don't want to see our stores sold.''

"But?''

"But," Jimmy said, "I have sense enough to take a once in a lifetime offer when it comes my way."

"So, the deal is that good?"

For a moment, Jimmy looked confused. "What deal?"

"There were three people from Heart at that secret meeting."

Jimmy grinned. "You got good intelligence. That always comes in handy in our business."

Cole had grown weary of the cat and mouse game. "So, are you going to tell me what the strategy is, or am I just supposed to guess?"

"Since I don't like your tone, you'll have to guess," Jimmy taunted.

Cole stood. "Fine, Uncle Jimmy. I'll see you next week."

Cole strode to the door leading to the small conference room, but Jimmy halted him before he yanked it open.

Cole sighed and faced his uncle. "Yes?"

"What I came to tell you today needs to be told. You're a grown man, Cole. I like you. Sometimes." he added. "If you don't already know it, you need to realize that everybody who purports to have your best interests at heart doesn't. Tread carefully, boy."

Cole looked at his uncle, then opened the door and rejoined his meeting.

Jimmy stood alone in Cole's big office. He looked around again at the Spartan decorations. Cole didn't have enough life in his life. As he stood there, Jimmy got an idea, and just for the hell of it he changed his mind about how he was going to vote at the meeting.

The Fourth of July was his favorite holiday. Nothing

like a few fireworks to liven up a party. Jimmy decided
to celebrate a little early this year.


After his meeting on the progress Sonja and Brian's
people were making in the stores, Cole had time to
think about first his mother's and then Uncle Jimmy's
odd behavior.

His mother had taken an instant and permanent dislike to Sonja. And Uncle Jimmy's presence in the office
was so out of the ordinary that Cole rehashed their
conversation over and over. The only thing he'd said
that made any sense was his parting advice. Cole knew
a warning when he heard one. He just didn't know who
or what Uncle Jimmy had warned him about.

Few people were in his corner, so in that regard his
uncle's advice about treading carefully met the preach-
ing to the choir standard. Treading carefully was SOP
for Cole—standard operating procedure—particularly
where his relatives were concerned.

After a while, Cole stopped worrying about his relatives and their cloak and dagger games. There was something more important to handle right now. He showered
and changed clothes at the office, then drove to Sonja's
house. They'd spent the last two weeks being practically
inseparable. While company business kept them
together in his office or at the stores most of the time,
Cole had managed to arrange a couple of real dates,
like the one they had for this evening.

Cole had made one request: That she wear the red,
backless dress he'd briefly seen her in many weeks ago.

In a teasing moment, Sonja responded, "How do you
know that's the best thing in my closet?"

Passion flared in his eyes. "If you can do better than that, I want to see it."

Sonja just smiled.

Cole's own mouth quirked as he recalled the conversation. He could only wonder what she'd wear. They hadn't been together intimately since that first time. Cole still wanted her. He wanted to linger in the lovemaking. To inhale her woman scent. To lose himself in her arms.

They'd kissed in the time since that first frantic night of joining, but Sonja always brought a halt to things before they went too far. The shy act she played heightened his awareness of her . . . and his need for her.

Tonight, Cole decided, things would end differently. He knew she wanted him. He'd seen his own desire mirrored in her eyes. He'd felt her gaze on him when she thought he wasn't looking. The soft, subtle scent of her had him hungry for the chance to bury his head in her neck, to lick the tender skin there, to run his hands through her hair.

Cole couldn't remember the last time he'd been out dancing. He didn't even know there were places *to* go dancing. But Sonja's suggestion suited his plans perfectly. During the slow songs he'd show her just how much his body ached for hers. Sonja's soft laugh when he asked about the slow songs reminded him that he'd been living a hermit's life too long.

Sonja was like no woman he'd ever known. She understood him, his language, his personality. She spoke to him on a physical and an intellectual parallel that had no equal.

Cole drove up her driveway and got out of his car. Before he took a step or shut the door, Sonja was coming

out of her front door. All of a sudden, he agreed with
Uncle Jimmy's crude assessment: Sonja was a hot piece.

His breath caught when he got a good look at her in
a tiny black dress. Strips of her bare skin flashed between
the sheer material that barely covered her breasts. She
wore stiletto heels covered with the same sheer material.
Cole tracked the line from her leg to thigh that beckoned and teased from the dress.

His arousal, swift and sure, didn't escape Sonja's
notice as she joined him at the car door.

"Is that a gun in your pocket, or are you just happy
to see me?"

Cole smiled at the old line. "Very happy to see you."

But he dared not move toward her, not right now
while blood roared through his veins and his heart
pounded. If this was what it felt like to have a heart
attack, Cole would willingly suffer the consequences.

Surely, that dress, what little there was of it, was illegal.
On one hand, he was sorry he'd challenged her. He
wanted to cover her in sackcloth so no other man could
see what he had. On the other, he wanted to flaunt her
sexiness all over the city. But mostly he wanted to hike
the short hem up and take her on the hood of his car.
They'd come together hard and fast, like that dress
demanded.

Cole wasn't at all sure that they'd ever get to the
dance. As a matter of fact, he wasn't sure he was going
to make it through the next few minutes.

"Sonja."

"Yes, Cole," she murmured as she sidled next to him.

Cole swallowed and clutched his hands into fists at
his sides. She rubbed against him, soft and slow and
easy, like a kitten getting comfortable. He groaned and

gave up the fight. Their kiss robbed him of breath, of sense, of reason.

Then, shaking with the want of her, Cole pushed her away.

"Sonja. You have to change."

"Excuse me?"

"You have to wear something else. I'm not very proud of the thoughts rolling through my head right now. If I feel this way, I don't want to think about how some other guy is going to react to seeing you in that."

Sonja's teasing smile told him she didn't believe how close to the raw edge he was. He'd been so long without her.

"Sonja, I'm serious. You can't go out like that."

"I'm already outside." She leaned into him, rubbing her pelvis against his crotch. She reached a hand down and stroked the hard length of his erection.

Cole growled and buried his head in her neck. "Let's go."

He half dragged, half carried her back along the cobblestone walkway to her front door. Once inside, Sonja's expensive little outfit met a swift and permanent demise. With her dress ripped in pieces and his trousers bunched about his hips, they made it as far as the carpeted stairs in her foyer.

# Chapter 14

"Sonja, we have to talk."

"We talk all the time. I'd rather do," she said.

Cole struggled to keep focused. Sonja's skin was still moist from the shower they'd taken. She sat at the vanity in her large bathroom and dabbed perfume from a stopper between her breasts.

He placed his hands on her shoulders, and Sonja leaned into the light embrace. Cole kissed her on the top of her head.

"Can we have this conversation somewhere else?"

Sonja chuckled. "Now you're talking."

"No, not there, either. How about the kitchen or the garage? Someplace neutral. We need to talk."

Sonja reached around, gently pulled his face to hers, and kissed him. "Okay, spoilsport. I'll get dressed and meet you in the kitchen."

Several minutes later, they sat in the sunroom off Sonja's gourmet kitchen. Microwave popcorn popped and coffee brewed. She leaned both elbows on the table and regarded Cole.

"So, what did you want to talk about?"

He took her hands in his. "Us. I want to talk about us. About this thing between us."

A shadow crossed her face. He wanted to talk about *that.* Sonja extricated her hands from his and struggled with the demons that rode her conscience. Why couldn't he just let things be?

"Can't we talk about something else?"

"Sonja, in the weeks we've been working together I've grown to care about you. You exemplify all the characteristics I admire in a woman. Your honesty and integrity, your spirit. I love how you're passionate about your company. You bring that same passion to bed. You make me feel alive, and I haven't felt that way in a long time."

"Cole, you're making me uncomfortable."

She got up and fiddled with the coffeemaker.

"There's nothing to feel uncomfortable about, Sonja. We're good together."

"Cole, I . . ."

She paused, trying to get her racing thoughts together. There he sat, all but declaring love for her. And all Sonja could think about was how quickly that tenderness would turn to anger once she told him the truth. Sonja had seen Cole on the warpath. It wasn't pretty for his victims or any innocent bystanders. He excised anything that didn't fit into his idea of what reality should be like a virus.

How, then, would he react if she blurted out the truth, the fact that she'd planned to let a potential rival know all of his stores' weaknesses? The fact that shopping the competition was standard operating procedure wouldn't fly very far, particularly in the face of her own duplicity.

She tried to rationalize away the guilt. Maybe Claiborne Bros. would make a counteroffer for the Heart stores. If that happened, Heart would be allied with a company of similar philosophy, one which had the bonus of being larger in scope and deeper in the pockets.

*Stop making excuses and looking for loopholes. Tell him the truth!*

*I can't.*

*Coward,* her inner self taunted.

Cole's arms wrapped around her waist. She hadn't even heard him approach.

"Sweetheart . . ."

Sonja flinched at the endearment.

"You look a thousand miles away. What's wrong?"

*Tell him!*

"Cole, I've done something I'm not proud of."

He smiled. "Hey, we all have. We're human. Want to hear my list? It's pretty long."

She bit her lower lip. "You don't understand."

Cole turned her in his arms and lowered his mouth to hers for a sweet taste. "Help me understand, then," he said.

Sonja opened her mouth, but no words came out. She stared into his eyes and wished she were a different person. She stared into his honest eyes and wondered why the fates had put them together.

*It wasn't fate. It was deception, and lust,* her conscience reminded her.

Sonja closed her eyes and shook her head.

"Honey, whatever it is, you can tell me. Tell me in

your own time and your own way. It doesn't have to be right now.''

She turned away from him and covered her mouth with her hand. How had she gotten in so deep, so fast? None of this was supposed to have happened this way.

"Sonja, will you let me keep loving you? You know how we are together. Look what happened tonight. Look at what happened the first time."

"I don't think that's a good idea."

"Why? We're terrific together."

"A relationship with frantic coupling as its foundation isn't going to last very long. Sex isn't the only part of a relationship. There has to be more than that, a lot more."

"And I say we have it."

Sonja shook her head.

"There's obviously a disconnect here." His response held more than a touch of irritation.

She seized on that. If he got angry, he'd forget all that nonsense about deep feelings. Sonja deliberately baited him.

"You're right. You want more than I can give. Stop pressuring me. I'm not one of your general managers."

Cole's lips tightened into a thin, disparaging line. "And it's a damn good thing, too. I'd fire you for being an inconsistent tease."

Sonja said the words she knew would hurt the most, but even as she said them she knew she would bleed more than Cole. "Why don't I save you the trouble? I'm firing *you*. Get out of my house."

Cole stared at her as if she'd grown two heads. Then, without a word, he stormed out of the house. Her front door slammed, then bounced off the stopper.

"Unlocked door is open. Unlocked door is open," her security system chimed.

Tears were falling by the time she made her way to the foyer to shut the door. The roar of Cole's engine and the screech of tires as he took off down the street told her how well she'd succeeded in making him angry.

It was for the best, she kept telling herself, but Sonja didn't believe that for one second. She stood in her foyer, then sank to a step in a heap of tears and regret for what might have been.

By the time the red haze of anger dissipated, Cole was in Richmond. He'd passed the Williamsburg exit to his house without even noticing. The powerful engine in his Lincoln Town Car could easily handle the abuse. Cole took an exit and drove around the city for a while, trying to figure out women.

"What's the use?" he wondered. He'd never understand.

The socialites his mother constantly put in his path begged for a tenth of what he had freely offered Sonja. And she threw his consideration back in his face. Fine. If that's the way she wanted it.

But as Cole headed to the apartment the company kept in Richmond, he wondered about the change in Sonja. She readily, even eagerly, slept with him and rocked his world in bed. Yet, when the talk turned to, well, talk, she freaked out.

By the time Cole made it to the building, parked his car, and got into the apartment, he was keyed up. He considered a walk or run or even a game of racquetball in the first floor court. But as he headed to the court and the locker room where he always kept a change of clothes, he decided to drive around the city some more. Still in his suit, he went back to the garage.

His destination came easily. He headed to the Heart store, one of three in the chain of eight that was a free-standing business. He drove the perimeter of the building. Then, with the motor running and his head-lights on, Cole sat in his car staring at the store.

It didn't take long at all for a cruiser to pull up beside him and flash a bright light at Cole's Town Car. Cole powered down his window.

"What's the problem, sir?" the officer asked.

Cole shielded his eyes from the light. "It's Cole Heart. Turn that thing off."

The guard moved the light out of Cole's direct line of vision but didn't extinguish it. Cole gave the guy points for being on his toes. He reached for ID and handed it to the guard.

"I own the place. You must be new."

Without saying anything, the guard shined his light on the driver's license Cole gave him. The guy still didn't look too convinced.

"I'm going to park over there, then use my keys to get in my store." The emphasis on *my* didn't even faze the security guard.

Cole requested his license back, then parked his car in a spot designated with a red heart. He let himself in a partially hidden entrance, then walked around his store. The future was a vastly unknown quantity, even with Cole's level of confidence. So he walked around, crossing through departments, straightening the occa-sional display, and contemplating his past and his present.

With the exception of a summer he spent as a camp counselor while in high school, Cole had never worked anywhere but in Heart stores. He'd done it all, too, on both the managerial and employee levels. Under his grandfather's guidance, Cole swept floors and cleaned rest room toilets. He'd been a stock clerk, an inventory appraiser, and a customer service representative working the credit department phone lines. He'd done stints in security and loss prevention, gift wrap, even sold womens' lingerie.

He had to prove himself in each area before his grandfather let him try his hand at the more glamorous positions like buyer, and promotions and event coordinator. Each time Cole realized he had a real aptitude for any one area, his grandfather sent him to another department to learn something new—accounting, returns, personnel.

Even though he sent every one of his children and grandchildren off to get fancy educations, the founding Heart believed a college degree wasn't worth the paper it was printed on. Nothing beat sweat and an honest day's work. Experience mattered. He recognized a protégé in his grandson, and wanted to make sure Cole knew every facet of the retail business.

Cole was doing the same thing with his nephew.

"Halt right there, buddy."

Cole turned and faced three city police officers with guns drawn. The security guard from the parking lot was there, too.

"You obviously didn't believe me," he told the guard.

"Hands in the air, bud. No fast moves," a cop said.

Cole complied. "My name is Coleman Heart the Third. I'm president and chief executive officer of Heart Federated Stores, Inc. My ID is in my jacket pocket."

"Get it. Nice and slow," said the cop in charge.

Having a head or two roll was Cole's first inclination

for handling the guard. Then he saw the humor in the situation. The guard was doing his job by the book. Cole could both respect and appreciate that dedication. He produced the requested items, as well as his Heart corporate identification badge.

As he leaned forward to hand them to the officer, he glanced at the security guard. "What's your name?"

The guard glared at him. Cole nodded.

"Uh oh," the cop stammered as he read the documents. He waved for the other officers to lower their weapons. "Mr. Heart, I'm sorry. We got a report of a suspicious man talking about breaking into the store."

Cole lowered his hands, accepted his ID from the city officer, then approached the still wary security guard.

Extending his hand, Cole said, "Cole Heart. How long have you worked here?"

The guard swallowed, glanced at the police officers, and then shook Cole's hand. "Three months, sir."

Cole nodded again as he assessed the young man. "College?"

"Graduate school, sir."

"Thanks for checking things out," Cole told both the officers and the private guard.

"Mr. Heart, next time you want to—"

Scurrying and huffing from the hallway interrupted, and got their attention. "What's going on here?" A harried looking man hurried forward. "Mr. Heart! What are you doing here?"

The man looked from Cole to the police officers and to the hired guard. "What's going on? Mr. Heart, are you okay?"

"Hello, Henry. I was just about to be arrested for breaking into the store . . . with my key," Cole added.

Before the store general manager could get another

word in, Cole held up a hand to halt Henry's verbal assault. "Just a sharp guard doing his job."

"Everything seems to be under control here. We'll leave. Mr. Heart, the next time you want to wander through your stores after hours, let somebody know ahead of time. You could have been shot."

"Shot?" Henry squealed. "What happened?"

Cole thanked the officers again for their quick response and shook hands with each one.

He paused at the guard. "I like your style. You played this completely by the book. Granted, you could have gotten me killed. That would not have been cool. What's your graduate degree in?"

"Business, sir. Are you really the head of Heart Federated Stores?"

"Yes, he's my boss. He's *the* boss," the general manager snapped. "Mr. Heart, I am so sorry. This will never happen again," he assured as he glared at the guard.

Cole ignored his GM and focused on the young man. "What happens after school?"

"I start looking for a job. I have another semester at Virginia Commonwealth University." The young man glanced at Henry. Then, steady and sure, he met Cole's gaze. "Am I out of a job now?"

"I should say so," Henry declared.

Cole listened to his gut as he made the call. In the man's eyes, stance, and face, Cole saw potential waiting to be matched with opportunity. Reaching into his inside jacket pocket, he pulled out a business card and handed it to the security guard. "Only if you'll consider another one. We have a management development program that might be of interest to you. That's my direct line. Give me a call, and we'll talk about it."

The guard thanked Cole and tucked the small card in a pocket of his brown uniform.

Cole saluted him with two fingers. "Carry on." Then, to the store manager, he added, "See you later, Henry."

Heading back up the aisle, Cole turned and called back to the guard. "What's your name?"

"Luis de Santos."

"Nice job tonight, Mr. de Santos."

# Chapter 15

Jimmy's conversation with Justine Heart had just the effect he intended: Justine's nerves lay frazzled and frayed as her past sins haunted her. She told Mallory that she had a quick shopping trip to make, then flew to Connecticut and rented a car for the long drive to a sedate mansion nestled in the countryside.

She hadn't been to the home in more than twenty years, and that last visit had been against her will. But now she felt compelled to make this visit. She needed to assure herself that she'd done the right thing.

Nervous, she parked the car and made her way to the front office, where she checked in. "I'm here to see Edwin Heart."

A receptionist in a bright yellow jacket ran a finger down a list, then glanced up. "He never gets visitors. Who may I say is calling?"

Justine's lips were pursed together. "His mother."

The two-week affair Justine had with Virginia Byrd's

fiancé, Coleman Heart II, resulted in a pregnancy. She wasn't supposed to get caught that way. Seducing Coleman had been about one-upping the snotty Virginia. But Justine found herself caught. In fear and desperation, she'd turned to Coleman's brother, Jimmy, for help. Jimmy Heart solved problems, and he'd always seemed friendly.

They planned for her to spend a year "studying" in Paris or Rome, birth the baby, and give it up for adoption. The only part of the plan they hadn't counted on was the baby being born with severe mental and physical handicaps. The adoption agency wouldn't take it, and Justine found herself stuck with an unwanted child.

The bargain she struck with Jimmy Heart seemed like a good idea at the time. She didn't know then that she was making a pact with a devil who would forever hold her indiscretion over her head. Jimmy said he'd find a home for the boy and make sure he was taken care of for life on the condition that Justine marry his brother, John. She'd flat out refused. Jimmy just shrugged and said "See ya." Realizing he was serious, Justine reviewed her options.

As Justine stood at the receptionist's desk waiting to be taken to see her son, she thought about the deal they'd struck. In exchange for her retarded son's care and Jimmy's silence, Justine would marry Jimmy's younger brother, John. If the marriage dissolved for any reason and under any circumstance except the natural death of John, Justine would inherit nothing, not a single dime. She'd be allowed to keep the clothes on her back and take one suitcase.

When she made the devil's agreement she'd been young and optimistic, sure that Jimmy was joking or would change his mind. He didn't. Not even when John

and Justine's relationship became so strained that they
lived on opposite wings of the large house the family
initially shared.

Many times during her loveless marriage, as she
watched Virginia and Coleman's union blossom, Justine
had wondered if her choice had been worth the price.
When Cole, the precious oldest male heir, was born,
Jimmy's smug look devastated her. Her son should have
been the one celebrated. Coleman's first son and true
heir was Edwin, not that damn Cole.

But no one knew about Edwin, no one except her
tormentor, Jimmy Heart.

Justine was led to a lounge decorated to look like a
cozy parlor. She stood there regretting just about every
aspect of her life. A heavyset man shuffled into the
room. His perpetual grin gave Justine chills.

"Hey," he grunted. "Me Ed."

The short visit upset Justine. She sat in her rented
Cadillac for a long time. Coming here had been a mistake, a huge mistake. Edwin's twisted features and vacant
grin frightened and repelled her. Edwin was the proof
of her wild past, a past she didn't generally think about,
let alone regret.

"Damn you, Jimmy Heart," she cursed, pounding the
steering wheel.

No one knew that when John died in a car accident
that the police deemed suspicious, all of his personal
wealth—every single dime, every house, and car—went
to Mallory, not Justine, as most people assumed. No
amount of pleading on her part had convinced Jimmy
that she hadn't tampered with those brakes.

For a long time, Justine had suspected that Jimmy's

handiwork was illegal. But she was too scared of losing everything to call him on it, and too embarrassed to see a lawyer about the situation. So Justine spent her life keeping up appearances for people she didn't even like.

She focused all of her energy on Mallory's long-term prosperity. Jimmy had been able to finagle the legalities of their deal, but he couldn't deny Mallory her rightful inheritance after John died.

But every quarter, like clockwork, Jimmy stroked a large check to keep Edwin ensconced safely away. For forty-two years, now, the secret checks had continued.

Mallory was wealthy in her own right. John was gone. Justine had nothing to lose by defying Jimmy.

"Nothing except your houses and cars and status," she said to herself. The status mattered most to Justine. She'd be a laughingstock if anyone knew her true circumstances. Unlike her sister-in-law, Virginia, Justine couldn't afford, literally, to alienate her daughter.

She glanced back at the big Georgian mansion that housed the rejects and cast-offs of well-to-do families. She shrugged off the melancholy and the guilt. Too much was at stake now for her to rock the boat in any way.

Edwin would be just fine. Justine started the car. She didn't plan to ever come back here.

Back in Virginia, Sonja was having her own pity party. How had it happened? How had she let herself get so emotionally involved with Cole Heart?

Her burden now weighed even heavier. Being honest with herself, she knew she had somehow, some way, fallen in love with the man. So miserable that she felt like crying, Sonja sat huddled in her big bed, already late to work. The day wasn't quite shaping up to be a banner one.

In just a few short weeks and a couple of quasi dates, she'd done the unthinkable. Even her focus had shifted. In the barrage of meetings with Cole and his management team, Sonja looked for and offered real solutions. She'd gotten caught up in the work and the moments, not to mention the man.

Her mother had always warned her that life had a tendency to play mean jokes on people. This one beat them all, though. Sonja reached for the telephone to call her mom, then realized she really didn't have anything to say. Her mother supported her in every endeavor and had always been Sonja's biggest cheerleader.

Edith Pride took things in stride, saying God and the law of the universe would see to the rest. Like the time Sonja had been cheated out of a scholarship. They'd desperately needed the money, and were overjoyed when the school counselor told Sonja she'd won. But a day later, the counselor came back, saying there had been a mistake, that the recognition had gone to a Heart. Shortly thereafter, the student newspaper reported that the school band was getting new uniforms courtesy of the Heart family.

Sonja didn't have to wait for God or anyone else to fix one of the wrongs she'd been about to perpetrate. She dialed her secretary and got the number for her contact at Claiborne Bros. Quickly, before she changed her mind, she called. After a bit of chit-chat, she got to the point.

"Thank you for considering The Pride Group," she told their marketing guy. "At this time, we'll be unable to supply the requested data on Heart Federated Stores.''

Explaining the why was a high hurdle. "Your business is one I would love to count among our clients, but I have a conflict of interest with regard to the Heart stores.''

She listened to the disappointed representative. Then she explained, to the best of her ability and willingness, why she couldn't in good conscience take Claiborne on as a client knowing they planned to seriously consider moving into the Hampton Roads market.

The call was one of the toughest Sonja ever made. Saying no to Claiborne was saying no a whole lot of money, plus any additional revenue that might be earned if Claiborne expanded. The representative from the chain left the door open for some sort of future partnership or working relationship. That gave her a little wiggle room, but nothing concrete.

Sonja finished the call and sat on her bed with the telephone in her hand, a digital voice reminding her to hang up.

Would Cole understand? How could she tell him what she'd done without confessing her original motivation?

"Doing what's right is always better than doing just because," she quoted her mother. Sonja repeated the advice like a mantra, wanting to believe it, hoping that Cole might see reason.

This time, when she picked up the telephone, she did dial her mom. Sonja, with shell-shocked nerves, found herself in desperate need of some mother love.

A week later and two days before the board meeting, Cole was looking forward to a rare evening at home.

Sonja claimed to be busy with another project, so his time was his own. He'd done everything he could do to prove to his relatives that he was the best man to salvage the Heart stores and lead them into the next century. All the calls had been made, the lobbying done. Each general manager was already implementing changes. Cole was confident that the meeting would go well. Sonja and her people had done a good job in a tight window.

The stores still had flaws, but with a permanent mystery shopping program in place, everyone from manager to janitor would be on alert to always think "customer first." The reward to employees caught doing right, cash and personal time, had been chosen by the general managers. Cole's dictum demanding immediate termination for those caught doing things horribly wrong had been met with skepticism and unease, until he reminded the managers about his own Heart experience as a mystery shopper.

Tonight, Cole looked forward to swimming in his pool and then practicing one of the stress reduction exercises his doctor had provided. He couldn't imagine sitting in front of a television any longer than fifteen minutes—the time it took him to get the business news from CNN. But the part about reading a novel or some other reading for pleasure had a bit of appeal. Cole caught snippets of books on tape, but couldn't remember the last time he'd read a novel.

So when Mallory showed up at his front door, he wasn't particularly welcoming.

"What brings you here, cousin?"

"We need to talk," Mallory said as she swept uninvited into a foyer large enough to sleep a family of six.

Cole couldn't claim to be very intrigued, but he did

wonder what had brought Mallory all the way to Williamsburg from her Virginia Beach retreat. The only other times she'd been here had been with his mother.

"You know, you've never shown me your home," she said. "Why a single man with no intention of getting married needs a house this huge is beyond me."

Cole still stood near the door. "If you want a tour, I suggest you look in the newspaper for an open house. This one isn't open for tours."

"Such a spoilsport."

Since she was already well inside, Cole closed the door then led her to a great room. Mallory spied a well-equipped wet bar.

"Nice," she said. "Mine isn't this big."

"What do you want?"

"How nice of you to offer. I'll take ginger ale."

Cole scowled and Mallory smiled. She knew full well he hadn't been asking her drink preference. But Cole walked around her and into the half kitchen. From a refrigerator tucked in the wall he pulled a can of ginger ale and handed it to her.

"No glass? No ice?"

"Mallory—"

"Let's not fight, cousin. We can save that for our board meetings. I've done a little investigating since our last one. I found out some interesting things, particularly about that consultant you hired."

Cole folded his arms.

Mallory smiled. "Oh, yes. I guess I should clarify which one. You do love your consultants."

Cole's patience thinned. "What is the point?"

"That Pride woman, the one who runs the little mystery shopping company? Interesting background she has. Did you check any of it before you cozied up with her?"

All the women in his family had a tendency to refer to Sonja as 'that Pride woman,' as if Sonja were a virus. "What do you have against Sonja?"

An elegant eyebrow rose, and Mallory smiled a wicked, little smile. "Oh, it's 'Sonja' now. I see. This is good, really good," she said, chuckling.

The sound reminded Cole of hyenas at play.

"Sonja has some interesting conflicts of interest," Mallory said. "You've been had, and you didn't even know it."

"If there's a point, I wish you'd hurry up and get to it."

Mallory smiled. "Okay, I will. Your Ms. Pride has a major axe to grind when it comes to our stores. The records show a lawsuit and a settlement, not to mention something else that I find highly intriguing and rather apropos."

"And what might that be?"

"All in good time, cousin. All in good time."

Given his mother's odd behavior about and around Sonja, his uncle's unprecedented advice and visit, and now Mallory's super smug look, Cole wondered if he'd missed some salient fact about Sonja.

"Don't you want to know about the lawsuit? At the heart of it, so to speak, are your father and Uncle Jimmy."

Cole didn't know anything about a lawsuit. He did know the method of operation of those two. Whatever carried his father's and Uncle Jimmy's fingerprints usually had trouble attached to it. He got a sinking feeling in the pit of his stomach.

"Seems the newspaper liked the situation so much,

they wrote three or four stories about it. One even made it to the front page. Would you like to see the clips, Cole? It's fascinating reading."

She pulled an envelope from her bag and handed it to him. Cole lifted the flap and saw photocopies of old newspaper stories. He flipped through them. One caught his eye: "Negro clerk says store chief made unwanted advance." A quick scan yielded the clerk's name—Edith Pride.

Cole folded the papers and closed the envelope. None of the sudden anxiety he felt showed in his eyes, his face, or his combative stance. "This looks like ancient history, Mallory."

Her smug smile did nothing for Cole's churning stomach. "You're right, cousin. It is," she said. She paused for a dramatic effect that grated on his nerves. "But we all know that people who don't know their past, have no future."

She placed her ginger ale on a table, then glanced around the room again. "Just thought I'd share that with you."

Mallory headed to the front door. Cole followed, glad to see her leave. As she opened the door, she paused.

"Hey, Cole. Remember when we were kids? I had the biggest crush on you. When I told my mother, she slapped me. She said I couldn't because you were my cousin. Mom said I could hate you, compete with you, or challenge you. But I couldn't love you like that."

Cole stared at her, wondering why everyone in his family decided to talk in obscure riddles of late.

"And the point of this nostalgia trip?"

"You know that bit about everyone having just six degrees of separation?"

Cole nodded.

Sonja smiled. "Sometimes it's not even six degrees. Goodnight, cousin. See you at work tomorrow."

All too readily, Cole closed the door. His curiosity about the old newspaper stories couldn't be contained any longer. The three stories didn't tell him a lot: Two clerks at the Hampton Heart department store claimed that the president of the company, Mr. Coleman Heart, had forced his attentions on them. The two, Edith Pride and Audrey Maxwell, sued Heart Federated—action unprecedented in the 1960's. According to the clips, the case was settled out of court for an undetermined amount.

Cole could only assume that Edith was Sonja's mother. The time was right. She kept telling him he didn't know her well enough to make and take certain liberties. Is this what she was talking about? Was she afraid that if he knew about the thirty-year-old lawsuit he'd see her in a different light?

Sonja's reticence to talk to him or discuss their relationship now took on greater meaning. Did she have, as Mallory claimed, an axe to grind? Or was she just embarrassed? Cole didn't know, but he did have to consider the source. Mallory had an agenda. She'd do anything that might give her a perceived upper hand, particularly right before a meeting that could determine all of their futures.

Before Cole could make it to the pool, his doorbell rang again. He tossed Mallory's envelope on a settee and answered the door. This time, it was his mother.

Had someone installed a "Do Drop In" sign at his drive?

"Good evening, Mother." He stepped aside to let her in. Virginia's smart gold pants suit complemented her figure and her complexion.

"I wasn't expecting you home. Mason said you'd left early. I thought you might have had a date."

"Fishing, Mother?"

Virginia *harrumphed* as she headed to the kitchen airing a laundry list of complaints about Justine, perceived slights at the enclave, and dire warnings for Cole. She didn't even realize Cole wasn't following.

Cole sighed as he shut the door. So much for his relaxing evening at home.

# Chapter 16

A crisis at the Raleigh, North Carolina store kept Cole unable to reach Sonja the next day. The morning of the meeting, he sat in his office staring at the soothing watercolor on his wall. The image of dawn, the only item in the office that remained from his father's reign as chairman, usually inspired him. In each new day existed the potential to excel, to grow, to make a difference. But on this day Cole saw very little to be excited about. In fact, he wished he had the power to turn back the clock, to make his last few days vanish.

Mallory's vaguely insinuating malice made a lot more sense after his mother's incoherent, hand-wringing tale of woe: Both of them were just crazy. That's where he'd like to leave the matter.

He *wanted* to believe that both his mother and his cousin were playing games with him. He wouldn't put that beyond Mallory. But the facts told a different story. Edith Pride's settlement with Heart didn't seem to be recounted anywhere in the company books. It had taken hours, but Cole spent the night poring through Heart's financial records.

Uncle Jimmy's peculiar form of accounting left a sour taste in Cole's mouth. "It's a wonder the two of you managed to keep yourselves out of jail."

His father and uncle's perfidy, financial and otherwise, wasn't a new thing. Sonja's was another story altogether.

What were the terms of that settlement? And what, exactly, had been at issue?

The more he thought about it, the angrier he became, and the angrier he became, the more he wanted to confront Sonja Pride. Sonja was the key to this.

Until yesterday, he'd convinced himself that he was actually falling in love. But on the short flight to Raleigh, when he had time to pick through the pieces of their so-called relationship, he came up short.

Sonja could engage him in conversation for hours, but what did they really talk about? Him mostly, Cole realized with a touch of chagrin. She remained pretty close-mouthed about herself, and had an artful way of ducking and dodging any but the most superficial queries about her own personal life. Several times, he now realized, she'd been about to tell him something but he'd cut her off with a kiss. What was it that he'd shut out simply because he couldn't keep his hands off her? What did she want to say?

Cole swore, then grabbed the telephone.

For the fifth time today, he called Sonja.

"I'm sorry, Mr. Heart. She's still in a meeting. I will let her know you've called."

He barely bit back the frustration that gnawed at him. "Tell her it's important that I see her. As soon as possible. Some rather disturbing information has come to light.''

Was she truly in a meeting, or was she hiding from him?

Swearing under his breath, he slammed the phone down. Something was wrong, really wrong. Every instinct and nerve ending in his body screamed danger, caution, alert. Cole just didn't know if the danger came from Sonja, from his mother, from Mallory, or from some other source.

Cole paced his office. Mason brought in a glass of water and an extra-strength antacid.

"They'll be here soon, Mr. Heart. The boardroom has been set up to accommodate everyone. Up to thirty people should easily fit.''

Mason knew the importance of this meeting. She knew what was at stake.

"You don't look as if you think the good guys are going to win,'' she said. "But it's going to work out the way it's supposed to.''

For the first time, Cole doubted his ability to pull this off. Too many unknown variables existed. Like what his aunt and cousin had been doing talking to Knight and Kraus. Cole hadn't been able to ferret out any additional information about their secret meeting, and it hadn't been for a lack of trying. Knight and Kraus still had a big interest in the Heart properties, but was otherwise being tight-lipped, which in itself was unusual enough to send Cole's blood pressure up several notches. He thought he'd had a cordial and open relationship with them.

"Being right doesn't always mean you win," he told Mason. "This is Round Two.''

"Do you think there'll be a Round Three?"

Cole shrugged. "Who knows. Is Lance here?"

"In his office, I believe. Want me to get him for you?"

"Yes." He changed his mind. "No. That's all right."

Mason slipped away and Cole stood there. He glanced at his watch then wiped his hands across his face.

The problem with being The Big, Bad Wolf was that no one ever got close enough to know the wolf's feelings. At thirty-five years old, Cole didn't have anyone he could truly call a close friend. In the weeks they'd worked together, Cole had told Sonja Pride more about himself than he'd ever told anyone.

He turned toward the phone. Then he sighed.

Here he was a mere two hours from the most important meeting of his life, and he didn't have anyone to root for him. No wife, no children, not even his mother, if her behavior at his house had been any indication. The conversation still rang in his ears.

Virginia had made it clear she wouldn't support him if Sonja Pride remained a consultant.

"What the hell does Sonja have to do with anything?"

"She has everything to do with it. If you weren't so blinded by whatever disgusting things the two of you do in bed together you'd know that."

"Excuse me?"

Virginia had the decency to blush, even though she looked as if she were about to throw up.

"Mother, I am tired of the games you and Mallory like to play. First she shows up with thirty-year-old news clips, and now you're standing here like a prima-donna—"

"Watch your tone, Coleman Heart."

Cole's patience had been pushed as far as it could go. "No, Mother. I won't. You, Mallory, and Aunt Justine want the world to revolve around you. Well, it doesn't.

If you're withholding information that I need to make intelligent, rational decisions about the future of Heart Federated Stores, I want that information now. So, for the last time, I'm going to ask you, what does Sonja Pride have to do with anything?''

"I'm not at liberty to say." Virginia sniffed.

"Then get out." He pointed toward the door.

Virginia slammed out of the house so hard that a pane of frosted glass in his front door cracked.

Instantly, Cole had regretted his words, but the damage had been done.

Still angry the next day, Virginia refused to take his call. From Raleigh, he'd had Mason order and send two dozen of his mother's favorite orchids.

With no significant other and no parental support, Cole stood alone.

Waiting had never set well with him. A man of action, Cole didn't take to moments of brooding self-reflection, but that's exactly what he'd been doing for the better part of the last hour. Disgusted with himself, Cole decided to spend the rest of the time before the meeting in the place he loved most.

"I'll be at the Hampton store until it's time," he told Mason on his way out the door. "I have the cell phone, and will keep it on."

She smiled and nodded, understanding etched on her face.

"Let me get this straight," Sonja said. "You're leaving The Pride Group to work for Ted Gallòne, and you think you're taking half my staff and the Robinson account with you? I don't think so."

Brian Jackson lounged insolently against the credenza

in Sonja's office. "What you think is of little consequence, Sonja. The facts are I don't need you, you need me. I'm the one who has made things happen around here. Without me, you're nothing."

Sonja stood her ground at her desk. "That overinflated sense of self is going to be your downfall."

He grinned. "That may be. But in the meantime, I get to watch yours. The Good Book says people perish without a vision. So it won't be long before The Pride Group languishes into obscurity. You shouldn't have blown Ted off. He's a visionary with great ideas."

"For someone who purports to be such a flame of creativity, drive and vision, it sounds as if you're headed off to be a lap dog."

She watched his eyes narrow and wondered how she'd let this situation blow up in her face.

"Better than being a bitch," he spit back.

She folded her arms and nodded. "Oh, now I get it. This is all because I wouldn't sleep with you."

"Now who has the overinflated ego? Don't think your little game has anything to do with this. I know how and when to separate business from other things."

"You're not taking any staff with you."

Brian rose and rolled his eyes. "As if you have anything to say about it. People quit all the time. You're just gonna have a lot of vacancies to fill all of a sudden. Good luck finding some quality people."

"If you're not out of this building in fifteen minutes, I'm calling the police."

His scornful laugh echoed through her office as he headed to the door. He paused there. "Hey, Sonja?"

"What?"

He gave her the finger, then sauntered away.

If Sonja hadn't been in control she would have thrown

something, preferably at her former friend and vice-president's head.

She had no one to blame but herself for this disaster. Giddy with success and one too many glasses of champagne, she had let a hug lead to a kiss one night. The kiss led to some heavy petting before Sonja had the presence of mind to put a halt to things. Brian had been trying to stake a claim and take liberties ever since.

"I should have fired his butt weeks ago."

But she hadn't. And now she found herself on the defensive and in what could be a precarious position with her largest client, a client she'd willingly handed off to Brian to cultivate, woo, and land.

Sonja swore.

"Stupid, stupid. How could you be so stupid?"

She buzzed her secretary. "Get me the Robinson account. Contracts, everything."

While she waited, Sonja called her attorney.

"Del, I have a situation that could blow up in my face. I may have to sue a former employee."

She told him who the employee was and gave him a summary of the ugly scene that had just transpired.

"When you said a 'situation,' you really meant a situation, didn't you? Do you have non-compete clauses in your contracts with your senior management team?"

"My senior management team consisted of my friends. When I started this company and brought them on board, we didn't have paper agreements. The contracts were oral."

It was the attorney's turn to cuss. "This is going to be a mess. But that's what I'm here for. Just call me the clean-up man. Okay, well, get me what you can on Brian, and let me know if any others defect."

A few minutes later her secretary came in with the

Robinson account information and a handful of paper telephone message slips.

"Cole Heart has called here five times in the last hour."

Sonja groaned. Men were starting to look like the bane of her existence. "Did he say what he wanted?"

"No. Just that it was imperative that he talk to you as soon as possible. I thought he was going to bite my head off through the phone."

"That would be Cole—Mr. In Touch with the People."

"Sonja, is it true about Brian? Is he really leaving to go work for Ted Gallòne?"

Reaching for the crystal paperweight on her desk, Sonja answered. "That's what he says."

"Well, that really sucks."

Sonja smiled. "Yeah, it does. Hey," she said, holding the piece of crystal to the light. "Were you ever able to find out who sent this?"

"No luck."

Sonja stared at the words *truth* and *integrity*. "That's too bad. I'd like to thank him or her."

Contemplating the words engraved on the paperweight every day had made her realize that she wanted to live and abide by those guiding principles. To do so, the first thing she had to do was come completely clean with Cole. She would tell him everything. If they got through that, she'd know they had a solid foundation.

"Anything else I need to know?"

"I've ordered some lunch for you. It should be here in about fifteen minutes."

Sonja smiled. "Thanks, you're a lifesaver."

"There are a couple of other people besides Cole Heart in the messages. Details are on the slips."

Sonja flipped through them then paused at one. Gal-lòne. He had a lot of nerve. Was probably calling to gloat.

She put her headset on and dialed Cole's private line. On the second ring, a cold ugly fact dawned on her: If Brian did steal or sabotage the Robinson account, she would need, would have to rely on that window the Claiborne people kept open. She'd need the Claiborne Bros. account. If push came to shove, would she compromise Cole's company to save her own? Claiborne was interested in the Heart locations. Cole's heart and soul were wrapped up in his stores.

"May I help you?" she heard a voice—Mason's?—repeat in her ear.

"Uh, sorry. Wrong number."

She sat there for a moment as the ramifications whipped through her head.

The shrill ring of the telephone jarred her. "This is Sonja."

"Hello, Ms. Pride. My name's Alex Andres, and I'm a reporter with the *Daily Business Journal*. I'm doing a story for tomorrow's paper and thought you might be able to help me. It's about infighting at Heart Federated Stores."

Sonja closed her eyes. Could this day get any worse?

Yes, it could. A lot worse. Cole watched his relatives file into the conference room, the battle lines clearly drawn. Lines of strain marked the eyes and the mouths of aunts and cousins who clearly didn't want to be in the middle of this conflict. Many of them had long ago given up any real interest in the company—except, of course, for the shareholder checks that landed in their mailboxes. In the last few years, though, those bank drafts had gotten smaller and smaller.

Cole realized that any backlash he got today would be a direct result of that personal wealth frustration, not any significant wish to dissolve or sell the stores.

Mallory and Justine had forced this unnecessary showdown.

Speaking of the witches. They didn't fly in on brooms, but the effect was no less dramatic. Morticia Addams would have killed for the black and white bat number Justine sported. And Mallory's dramatic black and red suit looked as though someone had scraped garishly long fingernails over skin, leaving jagged gashes of blood.

Cole stood at the head of the table. Mallory, his opposition, did as he'd expected and positioned herself at the opposite end. They nodded at each other.

Virginia swept in on a cloud of lavender silk. She greeted everyone in the room, pointedly ignored Cole, and took a seat next to Jimmy.

Cole's eyebrows rose, but he didn't say anything.

"Well, that's interesting," Lance said at Cole's side.

Cole glanced at his nephew. "Plots, I'm sure." His mother and Uncle Jimmy in coalition seemed something of a stretch, but reality had been suspended for a while now. Nothing surprised Cole anymore.

The excited buzz and family reunion atmosphere that usually heralded the start of Heart board and shareholder meetings had been replaced by a low hum of worry, of whispered conversations, as the factions rallied in the remaining minutes before Cole called for order.

When all the seats were accounted for, Cole opened the meeting.

"Thank you all for coming today," he said. "As you

know, Heart Federated Stores have been in business for fifty years. Five outstanding decades as providers of merchandise and apparel to the community.

"We are here today for a discussion—"

"And vote," Mallory inserted.

Cole's eyes blazed for a moment and then he reached for the control he'd need to see him through this meeting without doing bodily injury to Mallory.

"We'll be discussing options available to shareholders. Near-term revenue enhancements will be critically important to us in the coming months."

Mallory rolled her eyes. "That means we need cash fast," she translated.

Cole scowled at her. "We have the potential to develop and capitalize on our strengths while bolstering our weaker areas. For example, in customer service."

He droned on about projects and potentiality. Mallory interrupted again.

"Cole, please. These delaying tactics of yours are pathetic."

"That's enough, Mallory," Jimmy croaked from his seat. "Let the man have his say."

This time, Jimmy's role as referee statesman backfired.

"Seems to me," Betty said dryly, "we wouldn't be going through all these gyrations if you'd taken care of business in the beginning, Jimmy."

Bev spoke up. "I agree with Aunt Betty. As a family, we should be trying to figure out what went wrong back when, and fix that. Cole seems to be trying to unravel this mess."

With hands on hips, Mallory confronted her cousin. "Excuse me, Miss Bev. But you aren't even a real Heart."

A gasp went through the room.

In a heartbeat, Virginia was up out of her chair and flying toward Mallory. Lance moved to intercept her, but Virginia moved fast for a woman her age.

"You have a lot of nerve," Bev said, standing and kicking her chair back.

"Please," Mallory said. "You showed up out of nowhere one day. You don't have a rightful place at the table or the—"

Virginia was in Mallory's face now. "Or the what, Mallory? You're sitting there like Miss High and Mighty passing judgment on people, but you better have a talk with your mama about your own place before you start casting aspersions on Bev, or anybody else in this room. I consider Bev my daughter, and that's all that matters. Rightful place, my behind."

For a moment panic filled Mallory's eyes, and she glanced at her mother. Justine wouldn't meet her gaze.

"Oh, you thought nobody knew your little secret, huh, Jussie? Well, I know," Virginia said. "I've always known. Mallory wouldn't be such a haughty witch if she knew everything I know, would she?"

"Don't go there, Virginia," Justine warned.

"Mother, Aunt Justine. Sit down."

Both women rounded on Cole in unison. "Don't you tell me what to do."

Lance moved to guide a hand to his aunt's waist, figuring Justine would move more easily than his grandmother. But Justine slapped him away. Surprised at being hit, Lance turned toward her and just missed the blow Virginia sent Justine's way in his defense.

"Don't you ever lay a hand on my grandbaby."

Cole, Jimmy, and a few other men quickly moved to separate the women before more serious blows could be lobbed.

If Cole hadn't been so angry he might have had time to doubt his ability to run a meeting. This was the second one that had disintegrated into chaos.

Everyone talked and shouted at the same time, presenting views. Virginia and Justine were being held at opposite sides of the room. Mallory and Bev exchanged hostile looks. Uncle Jimmy pounded his palm on the table demanding order, but no one paid him any mind.

It took a good five minutes before Cole could get everyone's attention. He started to jump on the table but nixed that notion. Crashing a glass into an art deco wastebasket did the trick. At the sound of the cracking glass everyone shut up at once and turned toward him.

"People, we are here today to *discuss* the remote possibility of selling the company, not to start World War Three. How about we act like responsible adults?"

From her spot at the table, where she hadn't moved, Aunt Betty raised her hand.

Cole sighed. "Yes, Aunt Betty."

"Cole, I make a motion that we adjourn for the day and reconvene in a week, when cooler heads can prevail."

"I second—" someone started.

"Wait a minute," Mallory said. "This is just one more delay tactic. We came here to vote, and by God, we're going to do just that."

"What's your hurry, Mallory?" Cole taunted. "Did you make some unauthorized promises you might not be able to keep?"

She advanced on him. "Just shut the hell up, Cole."

He smiled. "That's mighty articulate of you. There's a motion on the floor."

Aunt Betty raised her hand again. "Cole, can I rescind my motion and reword it?"

Cole wanted to scream in frustration. "Yes, Aunt Betty."

"Well, I make a motion that we adjourn for the day and reconvene on Friday, when we'll have one item of new business on the agenda—a vote to stay or to sell."

# Chapter 17

*Daily Business Journal*
Story by Alex Andres
HAMPTON—June 10.

*The best way to describe the management of Hampton-based Heart Federated Stores, Inc. is to refer to the Hatfields vs. McCoy's, according to company insiders.*

*From that famous feuding come these analogies:*

*Johnse Hatfield and Rosanna McCoy wanted to elope. Heart Federated, according to sources, wants to elope with any like-minded suitor from a larger chain.*

*The bloody feud between the Hatfield and McCoy clans caused far-reaching animosity. At Heart, shareholders are bitterly divided over everything from the day-to-day operations of the company to its long-term direction. From squabbles over what kind of soda to stock in employee lounges to a major dispute over the findings of an outside consultant's review, the*

*Hearts make the Hatfield-McCoy feud seem like child's play,* sources said.

*Rapidly declining revenue has tensions on edge throughout the stores,* said a department store supervisor who declined to give her name. That fact was confirmed by two Heart managers, one of whom recently resigned after being put on probation following the consultant's report about servicing customers.

"They talk customer service at Heart, but nobody gives a damn, from the top guy on down," said Joseph Tracker, 43. Until last month, Tracker was a personnel supervisor at the Heart Department Store in Richmond.

The report that caused a ripple effect in the stores was completed by The Pride Group, a Hampton-based market research firm.

Sonja Pride, president, said Heart Federated is typical of chains its size. "Growing pains are common," she said.

The financially beleaguered chain of department stores was founded in 1948 by Coleman Heart. Today, the company is run by Heart's oldest grandson, Coleman Heart III.

CEO Heart, 35, could not be reached for comment.

James Heart, chief financial officer emeritus, said the company has been and "will continue to be a player" in the retail market.

Heart Federated is privately held. Shareholders include Heart family members and few outsiders. According to market analysts, that fact alone makes Heart a prime candidate for a takeover bid. All it takes is a few disgruntled relatives to drive a permanent wedge in a company's prospect for longevity. Heart has those disgruntled family members in abundance.

Insider speculation names Knight and Kraus, the popular upscale department store chain, as a possible savior for Heart. Other likely players include Grant & Howard, the Washington, D.C.-based sportswear company, and I Don't Have Anything to Wear, a women's apparel store founded three years ago

*by two Brown University roommates. Both companies have
expressed interest in expanding into the southeastern markets
and have used family-owned operations like Heart to increase
their own share in the marketplace.*

*"It's unfortunate that the business situation has sunk to
these depths," said a high-ranking official who didn't want to
be named. "Heart has been in the community too long to see
it ignobly disintegrate this way. Coleman Heart, who founded
the first store, must be rolling in his grave at the indignity of
the shameful infighting."*

*Not everyone believes Heart is destined for failure. Analysts
say the right vision and direction could make Heart a long-
term player in the retail landscape.*

*"It takes effective leadership and a commitment to core val-
ues, as well as a healthy margin, to succeed. An IPO could
infuse the company with the capital it needs to survive," said
Gray Stobergenson, a Wall Street analyst.*

*Company officials have said, however, that Heart's senior
management remains opposed to an initial public offering of
stock, maintaining the family-owned business is important.
Others say too much emphasis placed on that very aspect of
the company has it in trouble right now.*

*With eight stores, three in Hampton Roads, one in Rich-
mond, Va., two in North Carolina, and two in the Detroit
area, Heart is diversified enough to make a legitimate go at a
turnaround, said the inside source. Selling off the North Carolina and Michigan properties could be a step in the right
direction.*

*Shareholders were scheduled to meet this week to decide the
future of the company.*

Cole calmly folded and placed the newspaper on the
round table in his office. Then he kicked the table over

so hard it crashed into his desk. A marble-filled vase of cut flowers flew in every direction.

"I could kill the person who did this! Who the hell leaked this information?"

Lance swallowed. Mason came running. "What's wrong? What happened?"

Lance kept an uneasy eye on Cole. "I'll take care of everything," he told Mason. "Would you get maintenance over here to take care of the carpet, please?"

"Leave the damn carpet," Cole raged. "How could she do this to me? What did I ever do to her to make her do something like this?"

"Her who?" Lance asked.

Cole plucked the newspaper from the floor and flung it at Lance. "Sonja Pride. Who else?"

Lance lifted an arm to shield his face from the force of the flying papers, then let them fall to the floor.

"Cole, that's not Sonja's style. That article has Mallory's fingerprints stamped all over it."

Cole got in Lance's face. "Witch that she is, even Mallory isn't stupid enough to air laundry that would dry up her precious Knight and Kraus deal."

Cole couldn't imagine anyone else with an axe to grind.

"You have a point there," Lance conceded. "Mallory wouldn't put a deal in jeopardy."

"And I should have fired that incompetent Joe Tracker. What does he know about anything? Mason!"

She jumped. "Yes, sir."

"Did that reporter call here yesterday?"

"Yes, Mr. Heart. It was during the meeting. There were two messages on voicemail when we got out. You said not to bother you for anything."

"Except news that Mallory had been hit by a car," Lance said.

The attempt at a little humor fell flat. Cole wasn't in the mood to be trifled with. He was out for blood, and he wanted to taste it now.

Mason had seen her boss angry before, but never like this. "I left a message on your machine at home about the reporter."

If Cole even heard her, he didn't acknowledge it.

"Cole?"

He ignored Lance. "Get the editor of that rag on the line. He needs to teach his little eager beaver reporter about facts."

Mason ran to his desk. "Yes, sir," she said, snatching up the telephone.

Cole kicked a chair out of his path. With all the things going on right now, the only thing that made any sense at all was the one thing that didn't: How Sonja was factored into the scenario. Cole knew all about inside sources. He'd been a victim of them once before. The reporter's story was too smug, too pat. His information could only have come from someone intimately familiar with corporate activity in the last couple of weeks. He'd given the board a summary of The Pride Group's confidential report. The reporter's article read as if he had a copy of one of the slick reports, a copy that could only have come from one source.

He couldn't believe that Sonja would betray him this way. But there it was in black and white, for a million people to read about. It was time to get to the bottom of whatever game she was playing.

"And get Sonja Pride in here. No, better yet, I'm going to her."

                          *   *   *

"Lord, have mercy, that story is a piece of work,"
Edith Pride told her daughter.

Sonja couldn't believe her eyes when she'd read the
paper. *The Daily Business Journal* was part of her everyday
reading, just like the local and regional newspapers.
She'd been on edge since talking to that reporter.

As it turned out, he used the one and only quote
she'd given him. Sonja refused to badmouth Cole or
Heart Federated. That's obviously what the reporter had
been looking for, though.

"Those anonymous sources can do a number on
you," Edith said. "I remember when word got out that
Audrey and I were taking on Heart. The newspaper
reporters had a field day. It was unheard of in that day
to sue somebody for sexual harassment."

Edith chuckled. "It didn't even have that name. Now-
adays, that's practically the only kind of story in the
news."

The two sat in Edith's comfortable living room. With
one foot tucked under her, Sonja nestled in her favorite
floral print wing chair. She'd taken the morning off to
work on a personal project and get her head cleared.
With her business life in turmoil, Sonja found comfort
and relief in the familiar: her mother's pancakes and
sausage, and work she enjoyed.

Cole had called about one hundred times yesterday.
His messages sounded increasingly cold, even hostile.
After her confrontation with Brian, Sonja had no desire
to take on another headstrong male. Once at home, she
turned off the ringers on the telephones and
retreated to her Jacuzzi.

Sonja had an idea for Cole, one that she could present

to him as she apologized for her initial deception. She let the soothing water organize her thoughts about that idea while it relaxed her tense body.

Edith stretched one leg out on the sofa.

"I tell you, the more things change the more they remain the same."

"How so?"

"Those Heart men can duck reporters, that's for sure."

Sonja felt a stab of guilt. She hadn't told her mother about her relationship with Cole Heart. Edith's disdain for the Hearts was no secret. At first, Sonja didn't know *how* to tell her mother. Now she wasn't sure she should, at all.

"What do you mean?" she asked.

Edith chuckled. "The Cole that's running things now conveniently couldn't be reached, according to the story. That's just how his Daddy was. He never had anything to say, so I made sure he always had a reminder."

"Mama, what are you talking about?"

Edith stared at the newspaper in her hand, then tossed it to the coffee table. She looked at her daughter and then sighed.

Alarmed, Sonja sat up and planted both feet on the floor. "What? What is it?"

Edith sighed again and sat up. Clasping both hands between her knees, she looked at her daughter.

"Well, I suppose enough time has passed. That devil is dead and gone on to his reward now, so what's the harm?"

"Mama, you're making me worry. What are you talking about? What devil?"

Edith expelled a shaky breath. "Well, you know

Audrey Maxwell and I sued Coleman Heart. He kept pestering us about dates.''

Sonja nodded. She knew all of this.

"He'd pat my behind or cop a feel on Audrey. She was real heavy-chested and self-conscious about it, too. He felt Audrey up one too many times. And me, well, he did things to me that . . ." Edith paused, swallowed and glanced at Sonja. "I always told him to stop, but he just said I was playing coy."

A trickle of uneasy awareness pricked Sonja.

"Anyway, we got ourselves a lawyer, well, really a lawyer-in-training—and filed a lawsuit. Nobody took us serious. I think Heart and that brother of his figured the case would be thrown out of court long before it ever got to a judge. But it didn't happen that way. We had a court date set. Their lawyer got nervous. When he got nervous, Coleman Heart got nervous."

"Why?" Sonja asked.

"Because we weren't the only ones. There wasn't a decent-looking female salesclerk in the Heart stores that one or all of those Heart boys hadn't chased. Some, of course, didn't mind. Some of us were disgusted. The rest were too scared that they'd lose their jobs to do or say anything. We tried to get a class action suit going, but it didn't work. Audrey and I were the only ones willing to stick our necks out."

"And you ended up settling the case."

Edith nodded. Then she got up. "Come with me."

Together, they went to Edith's bedroom. She motioned for Sonja to sit on the bed while she rummaged in the closet. She came out with a battered old hatbox. Edith took the faded green top off and searched until she found what she was looking for.

She handed Sonja a bankbook, its cover frayed with time and use.

"What's this?"

Edith looked at her daughter. "That's how you went to college."

Sonja's gaze shot to her mother's. Then she opened and flipped through the old checkbook. In her mother's precise handwriting were hefty and regular deposits and notes about interest. Eventually, the deposits stopped. The dates jumped several years and the notations turned to payments, all to Sonja's alma mater.

Edith pulled a sheaf from the box. "A condition of the settlement was that we couldn't talk about it. I didn't have a problem with that. I just wanted to send a message to Coleman Heart."

"What was the settlement, Mama?"

"Cash." She nodded toward the bankbook. "I got enough to get you through most of college. I figured that was the least Coleman Heart could do, given how much of my life he destroyed."

Edith handed Sonja the papers, clipped together with a large, rusted paper clip. Sonja eyed the packet with trepidation. She wasn't at all sure she wanted to know what the documents were. The uneasiness she felt turned in her stomach like bad milk.

"What's this?" she finally asked after gathering her courage.

"That's your legacy." Edith shrugged. "It's not much, but it's better than nothing."

Sonja took a deep breath and lifted the first page, then the next, and the next.

"Private stock certificates?"

Edith nodded. "Audrey and I wanted the Hearts to pay. Not just cash, but to pay with interest in their precious company. We got cash, and we got interest in their business.''

Sonja sat on the bed, stunned. "You're a shareholder in Heart Federated?"

Cole had said that there was some outstanding stock, owned by people not in the family, but that her mother—who hated the Hearts—was one of them was just mind-boggling.

She flipped through the agreements. "How much?"

"How much what?"

"How much interest do you own in Heart?"

Edith shrugged. "I don't own them. You do. I put them in your name years ago. It's five or six percent. Not a lot. Audrey opted for more cash than I took, so her portion was a lot less. I haven't talked to her in years. I wonder if she's still in this area."

Sonja opened her mouth to speak, but no words came out. They were all too busy racing through her head. *She* owned a stake in Heart stores? Cole's stores? The very thought was extraordinary. Absolutely unbelievable.

Then she realized something. Cole was in a life or perish struggle to keep his company. Every little bit would help. If she gave him her stock or her vote, it might put him a little closer to winning. Despite her initial goal to see him ruined, that was the very last thing she wanted now. Cole loved his company. He believed in the service and the people. Sonja had the power to help him—even if in this small way.

"Mama, you said these are mine?"

Edith nodded.

"Do you mind if I take them?"

"Not at all. Actually, I'm glad to get that mess out of my house."

Sonja leaned over and kissed her mother on the cheek. "There's something I need to do. Are we on for dinner on Thursday?"

"As always."

Grinning from ear to ear now, Sonja made a dash for the door.

"Do you see what that woman did? Do you see?" Virginia waved the newspaper in Cole's and Jimmy's faces. "I told you no good was going to come of this. It's just like last time. She doesn't get her way, and she goes running to the newspaper."

His mother and uncle had gotten to him before Cole could make it out the door to head to Sonja's. Now, he paced the boardroom with a pounding headache. The water suction and blower brought in by maintenance had chased him from his office, So Cole sat in one of the big leather chairs, wondering when he'd wake up and find himself back in control and enjoying his life.

"Last time, what? What are you talking about, Mother?"

Virginia clammed up and cast stricken eyes at Jimmy.

Jimmy sighed. "Cole, sit down. This is going to take a while."

"I don't have a while. I need to see Sonja."

Jimmy and Virginia exchanged glances.

"That's what we want to talk to you about," Jimmy said. "I'm going to ask you something and I need a straight answer, okay?"

Cole didn't say a word. Jimmy took that as the go-ahead.

"Have you had sex with Sonja Pride?" Jimmy asked.

Cole stood up. "I have *had* it with these questions

about Sonja. Either somebody tell me the whole truth, or I'm out of here.''

Virginia winced. "The whole truth?"

Cole shook his head and made for the door. "Good day, Mother. I have work to do."

"Not so fast, Cole. You're like Pops in that regard. Once you put your mind to something, that's it."

Folding massive arms at his chest, Cole stared at his mother and uncle. "Is there a point to this conversation?"

"Your daddy had a thing for the ladies, you know that," Jimmy said. "Sonja's mother, Edith Pride, took his fancy. She was working the fragrance counter in those days. When she finally realized he wasn't going to leave his wife, she sued him and the stores, claiming he'd sexually harassed her and another clerk."

A rock the size of a baseball settled in Cole's stomach. They couldn't be saying what he thought they were saying.

"Coleman, do you remember how upset you were when you found out Bev was your half-sister?" Virginia said. "You yelled at your father, screamed at him for not honoring me. Do you remember that day?"

His throat completely dry, Cole could only nod.

Virginia glanced at Jimmy, who nodded slightly, giving her the encouragement she needed right now.

"The affair your father had with Bev's mother wasn't his first, or his last. And she's not the only child he had with other women. She's just the only one I've ever accepted or acknowledged."

He knew. He'd known this was where all the games and the hints were leading. He'd known but he didn't want to believe it. How could Sonja, a woman he'd come to love, be . . .

Ice and dread coursed through Cole. A raw, primitive grief assailed him. And then, nothing. No emotion. No anger. Nothing.

Uncertain what to make of his non-reaction, Virginia reached a hand out to her son. "Coleman?"

He snatched his hand away. Unlikely tears brimmed in Virginia's eyes. "Coleman, we, I thought it best. . . ." Her voice trailed off.

Cole's gaze bored into Jimmy's and then his mother's, searching through their easy lies and half-truths, searching for any truth but the one they presented.

A quiet, deadly calm, like the moment before a bad storm hits, settled over the room. Cole's silence stretched. He watched his mother and uncle exchange uneasy glances. The only honorable Heart in the family had taught Cole to trust his gut, to rely on his own sense of being when faced with difficult decisions and moments.

Cole stared at his mother and uncle then took a big leap of faith. Without regard to the evidence, he trusted his gut.

"I don't believe you."


Mallory and Justine sat at a table in the crowded hotel restaurant. They'd come to celebrate. At lunchtime, the place was crowded with many of the lawyers, paralegals, and office workers who filled downtown each day.

They each held a glass of champagne. "To good work and hungry journalists," Justine said with a smile.

"To the millions we'll get from Knight and Kraus," Mallory toasted.

They sipped from their glasses, then regarded the *Daily Business Journal* article again.

"I can't believe that stupid little Pride woman said anything at all to that reporter."

"Why not? She *was* set up to take the fall. And Cole will, of course, jump to conclusions," Mallory said. She sipped from her glass and frowned. "I am, however, concerned about the tone of the whole thing, Mom. Particularly the part where he speculates on possible partners. That's not information we wanted public."

Justine waved the issue away with a well-manicured nail. "Not to worry. We can call with another insider tip, downplaying that part while making that Pride woman look like Deep Throat."

Mallory smiled. But she wondered if this time her mother had gone too far overboard in her zeal to hurt Cole. Mallory wanted to win, and she knew she could with what Knight and Kraus promised. But this article could do damage that even she couldn't spin.

# Chapter 18

"Cole, there's something I need to tell you."

"Good," he said, "because I want to talk to you about the DBJ article, among other things."

Sonja didn't at all care for the belligerent bully tone of Cole's voice on the telephone. "Is there a problem?"

"You tell me," he cut back.

Sonja cocked her head and stared at the telephone for a moment. "We obviously need to talk."

"I'm on my way," he said.

By the time Cole got to her house Sonja had worked herself into a semi-fury. The fact that her own guilt propelled her anger didn't help matters.

She opened the door to let him in. The scowl on Cole's face could have scared small children. But Sonja wasn't a child, and as usual she refused to be intimidated.

He didn't seem inclined to go beyond the foyer, so

Sonja stood there, marshaling her defenses in the face of his controlled anger.

"I don't know what has you all worked up, but let me tell you this," she said, "you need to understand I am not one of your little flunkies who you can order around at your whim."

"Of course not," he muttered. "That would be too easy."

"And I don't take well to sarcastic and cutting remarks in person or on the phone."

When he simply glared at her, Sonja sighed. "Cole, what do you want?"

"I've been trying to reach you. You've been conveniently unavailable."

"My company does one job for you, we sleep together a couple of times and you think I'm supposed to be at your beck and call twenty-four seven." She shook her head and rested her hands on her hips. "You've got an ego the size of the Grand Canyon, pal."

He advanced on her, but Sonja stood her ground.

"It's not about ego, baby. It's about loyalty. At least I can expect some measure of loyalty from my people. I thought I could count on it from the woman I have an emotional bond with."

Sonja's heart lurched.

Was he declaring something? Did he feel the same confused but exhilarated way about her that she felt about him? "What did you say?"

"I thought I could trust you."

His cold, flat words deflated Sonja's euphoric bubble. He didn't love her. He didn't even like her, let alone trust her. He had good reason to distrust her, but not for the reason he seemed to be steamed about right now.

"Excuse me?"

Cole swore. "Come off the innocent act, Sonja. It's wearing kind of thin. I thought you were on my side. I thought you, of all people, understood me."

"I see I've been tried and convicted, and here I'm not even sure about the charge. Care to enlighten me?"

With arms folded across her chest and her heart secretly aching, Sonja stared, and dared him to articulate his grievances against her.

In the face of her absolute certainty, Cole faltered. What if Sonja were the victim, not the perpetrator? He knew but one way to find out.

"Were you the anonymous source, the high-ranking official in that news article today?"

"No, Cole. I wasn't."

"Did you give that reporter a copy or a summary of your findings?"

"I did not."

For a long moment, they stared at each other; he, divining the truth from her eyes, Sonja willing her innocence on this point be conveyed.

Eventually, Cole closed his eyes and his shoulders slumped.

"I don't know who or what to believe anymore."

"I listen to my inner voice," Sonja said. "It's been nagging at me for a while."

Cole shrugged out of his suit jacket and draped it over the knob of the banister. He loosened his tie.

"Want some coffee?" she offered.

"Yeah. Sounds good."

He followed her to the kitchen. A few minutes later, Sonja settled on a sofa in the great room and Cole sat in a facing chair.

"I went to your office. I had a surprise for you. But

everyone was gone. The guard said the corporate offices were closed for the rest of the day. What happened? I thought you had the big meeting."

"We did."

Sonja leaned forward. "So don't keep me in suspense. What happened?"

Cole wanted to believe the best of Sonja, but his relatives had done a number on him. He'd go to his grave before ever admitting it to any one of them, but they'd managed to plant just enough doubt to make him edit his comments to Sonja before he voiced them. He'd come to enjoy arguing strategy with her. He liked her wit and her take no prisoners outlook. Sonja would have found something positive in the shareholders' meeting. In Cole's estimation, it was an unmitigated disaster. If the catfight hadn't erupted between the aunts, Cole might have been able to keep the proceedings on track and in check.

He gave her a summary of the meeting then made a mental note to have extra security at the enclave Friday. The way they went at it yesterday, it wouldn't surprise him if someone packed heat at the next meeting. Sonja's wince confirmed for him exactly how bad things had been.

Cole didn't know that his every word sent Sonja a little deeper into doubt. If she came clean now, she figured he'd assume the worst—which was probably pretty close to what she'd planned.

*Tell him the rest,* her conscience nudged. *Tell him before it's too late.* Sonja took a deep breath.

"Cole, I've done some things I'm not proud of. They concern you.

A shadow crossed his face. "What?" Before Sonja

could answer, Cole's pager went off. He checked the number and swore.

"Where's your phone?"

Sonja stared at him. His arrogance riled her anger again. "Sure, Cole. You may use my telephone," she said sarcastically. "It's over there."

The subtlety was lost on Cole. "I left my cell phone in the car charging up."

He made his call, argued at length with the person on the other end. Then, with a quick apology, muttering about timing, he was out the door.

Sonja stood staring at the spot where a moment ago she'd been about to confess.

"Looks like you've missed your chance, again, bud."

Friday dawned overcast. The gray pall hanging over the city cloaked Cole's optimism. Too tense to sleep, he'd spent the night in his study reading his grandfather's guidelines on how to run a successful business. Pops had passed the two leather journals on to his son, Cole's father, who promptly tossed them in a trunk.

One day while in college, Cole had found the volumes and read them cover to cover. He learned from his grandfather's mistakes and advice. He wondered why his own father had ignored the same wisdom.

"Old-fashioned ramblings," Coleman II declared as he signed the authorization for yet another remodeling job at one of the stores. They spent a lot of money on remodeling. Yet, in Cole's estimation, the stores always looked the same.

Cole spent the night before the vote reading the journals, reacquainting himself with the words that had always inspired and strengthened him. His own father neglected to recognize the value in the guidelines. Cole recognized the inherent value, and he understood the challenge in the simplicity. The straightforward advice made so much sense, even now, fifty years after that first Coleman launched his small dry goods store: Good product + good service = good customer. Good customer + good Heart experience = satisfaction and good will in the community.

Customer. Service. Community. Those guiding principles had launched the company, and would see it into the future. Cole's innovation, along with the customer service program and training Sonja helped launch, would steer Heart back in the right direction.

He donned his battle armor, a dark blue suit and a gray and red tie. When he arrived at the enclave, Mason was decked out in black.

"It's not a funeral, you know."

She glanced at her dress. "It's so yucky outside today that I couldn't muster the energy. You had a call."

"This early?"

Mason nodded. "A Luis de Santos. He said you told him to call. He works in the Richmond store."

Cole smiled. "He's the one who almost had me shot."

Mason's gasp made Cole chuckle. "He was just doing his job. What'd he have to say?"

She handed him a glass of juice and a small pill. "He'll be in Hampton this morning, and wanted to know if he could make an appointment to see you."

Cole glanced at the pill. "How do I know you're not feeding me poison every day?"

Mason didn't miss a beat. "If I were going to knock you off, there'd be nothing subtle about it. I'd just tell you, and then I'd do it."

Cole chuckled. "Put de Santos down for ten."

"Already done. I told him to arrive by nine-thirty."

He shook his head. "You sure you're not related to Radar O'Reilly?"

She just smiled.

Four hours later, no one smiled as they filed into the Heart boardroom. The table and chairs were set to accommodate everyone. With the exception of Mason, who was there to record the proceedings, every person in the room from teen to senior citizen would vote his or her percentage. Cole looked around, counting the votes he knew he had, the ones he could forget about, and the swing votes, like his mother's, that had kept him awake all night.

The meeting with de Santos had gone well. So well, in fact, that Cole had the guard stay to work the meeting. If fisticuffs broke out again, at least there would be some backup.

A commotion at the door caught Cole's attention.

"And just where do you think you're going?" Virginia Heart shrieked.

"I have every right to be here, Mrs. Heart."

Sonja?

Cole left his place and strode to the door. Luis stood between the women. "Mr. Heart?"

"It's okay. This one is my mother. This one is my . . ."

Sonja and Virginia waited for his explanation.

"She's okay," Cole finished.

Luis stepped aside.

"Really, Cole, an armed guard. Don't you think that's a bit excessive?"

Cole ignored his mother's complaint and turned his attention to Sonja. "What are you doing here?"

"I'm a shareholder. I'm here to cast my votes."

"Don't be ridiculous," Virginia scoffed.

Jimmy Heart shuffled up at that moment. He looked at Sonja and Cole, then at his sister-in-law. "Chickens coming home to roost this day."

After that cryptic remark, he faced Sonja. "You favor your mama," Jimmy said.

Cole's eyebrows rose. "How do you know her mother?"

"It's not her mama you need to be concerned about, Cole. It's her daddy," Jimmy said. Then, over his shoulder to Cole and the guard, he added, "Let her in. She has every right to be here."

With another pointed glance at Sonja, Jimmy took Virginia by the elbow and led her into the boardroom.

It was out and said now, the very thing Cole couldn't bring himself to face last night. It was the only thing that really mattered. Sonja wouldn't meet his eye. She stepped by him and walked into the room. She registered with the secretary and took a seat at the table.

Cole knew he presented the picture of calm and confidence. His secretary obviously knew him too well, and must have noticed his distress. Right before he brought the meeting to order, Mason slipped four small chewable tablets into his hand. Cole downed the antacid, took a sip of water, then asked everyone to be seated.

Cole made a passionate statement about family values and the company's rich past. Mallory's rebuttal encouraged the family members to look forward instead of backward.

Too soon, it was time.

The motion was made, the question and discussion done with. A vote to hold would be in Cole's favor, votes to sell would be in Mallory's.

Mason began the roll call and the tally. Cole started by voting his shares to hold. After the extended family members cast their choices the count was close, with a slight edge in Mallory's favor. Cole's stomach churned. He could pull this off, he knew it. The bulk of the interest was held by four factions: Cole and his mother, Uncle Jimmy and his family, Justine and Mallory, and Aunt Betty's family.

Sonja sat on the edge of her seat. Cole stood impassive.

"James Heart," Mason called.

Jimmy stood up. "I want you all to know that I haven't made my choice lightly. In the last several months, I've seen some things that have made me ashamed of myself and my family and my stores. It's time we do something about that. I am voting my percentages and proxies for my wife and three children."

He paused dramatically. Every eye in the room was on Jimmy. He thrilled at the power. Then he glanced at his CEO nephew.

"I'm sorry," Jimmy said.

Mallory smiled broadly. Cole stared straight ahead, seeing through the uncle who had given him nothing but a hard way to go.

"Our votes are to hold," Jimmy said.

Excited chatter filled the room. Cole let out the breath he hadn't realized he was holding. Mallory's mouth dropped open then snapped shut.

"Cole, I don't always agree with you. But I think you're the man to get us over." With that ringing and historic endorsement, Uncle Jimmy winked at Cole and took his seat.

"Oh, and by the way. It wasn't me at that secret party over to Knight and Kraus," he added.

Cole nodded, and Mason moved to the next names on her list. Bev and Lance cast their few shares with Cole. Lance looked at Cole, silently apologizing for not having more to leverage with.

Mason recorded the votes and called the next shareholders. "Justine and Mallory Heart."

"We vote our percentages to sell," Mallory said.

Then, as Cole knew they would, Aunt Betty and her crew voted to defect.

Cole's head was pounding at this point. He refused, however, to massage his temples or in any way show his tension. His mother was next. Cole stared at her, wondering what would come out of her mouth.

"I love my son dearly," she began.

Cole waited for the "But." With Virginia there was always a but clause.

"But I don't always agree with him. For more than thirty odd years I have done nothing but go with the flow. First, it was with my husband's wishes, and later with my son's. Well, from now on, I'm voting my conscience. And my conscience says it's time to let new blood deal with the stores. My vote is to sell."

A cheer went up on Mallory's side of the room.

Cole felt as if he'd been hit with a steel wrecking ball.

"And for your information," Virginia added, "I was the third person at that not-so-secret meeting. Knight and Kraus has an excellent plan to—"

His voice flat and void of any emotion or rancor, Cole said, "Save the lobbying for later, Mother. We're in the middle of a vote.' "

Virginia sat down, but not before glaring at her son.

Mason called Sonja Pride next.

"My mother and I own five percent of Heart Federated," she said. She glanced at Cole, but he refused to meet her gaze. He stared straight ahead. "Our percentage votes are cast with Cole. We vote to hold."

Not a flicker of emotion came from Cole. Mason called the next outside shareholder. Two other outside shareholders cast their split lots, one vote on each side.

"All eligible shareholders have voted in person or in proxy," Mason said. "One moment while the tally is made."

But Cole had already done the math.

Mason looked up. Cole nodded and she rose.

"Votes to sell, fifty-two percent. Votes to hold, forty-eight percent."

Mallory's and Justine's cheer rang though the room.

Sonja looked stunned.

Jimmy sat back in his chair and chewed on his unlit stogie.

Lance and his mother whispered together.

Virginia looked everywhere in the room except at her son.

Cole took a deep breath. He had never known such abject, total emptiness. He stared at his relatives, wondering if any of them realized what they'd just given away.

In the heartbeat of silence after Mason read the totals, he tried to remain objective. He attempted to convince himself that it wasn't personal, it was just business. But Cole knew that to be a lie. Today's vote was a slap in his face, the no-confidence vote Mallory had been itching for from the moment he'd been named CEO.

He took a deep breath.

"The votes have been cast and tallied. Shareholders of Heart Federated Stores, Inc. have decided to sell the collective holdings. Thank you to those of you who recognized and believed in the vision set forth by our founder.''

Cole looked each person in the room in the eye, lingering at his adversaries: Mallory, Justine, Aunt Betty, his mother. He saved the longest stare for Sonja, then he addressed the entire group.

"My resignation as chairman of the board of Heart Federated is effective immediately.''

He picked up his portfolio and walked out of the room with his head held high.

For a moment, no one said or did anything. Then, everyone spoke at once.

"I didn't want him to quit. Who's going to shepherd us through this?''

"Now we can stop dumping money into these dinosaurs.''

"What happens now?''

Lance and Sonja glanced at each other, then raced after Cole.

Mallory called for order and began to review the highlights of the Knight and Kraus proposal.

In the hallway, Cole leaned against the wall trying to get his bearings. It had been a long, long time since he cried, but he sure felt like doing it right now.

"Cole?''

He pushed himself from the wall. "We have nothing to discuss, Sonja. Go back to wherever you came from.''

"I understand your anger," she said. "I'm angry, too. Particularly when I think about what might have been.''

Cole stared down at her—six foot, three inches of solid, angry man. For the first time, Sonja felt like a pipsqueak next to him. She was glad she had the sturdy wall of Lance guarding her rear.

"Lady, I don't know what your game is supposed to

be, and I don't care. You know what? I don't even want to know who you really are. I'm sick of living knee deep in lies and half-truths. So just take yours and get out of my life.''

Lance anxiously looked from his uncle to Sonja, who clearly looked as if she were going to fall apart any moment. "Cole, I think you're making a mistake.''

Sonja touched Lance's arm, an intimate gesture that wasn't lost on Cole. "It's okay,'' she said. "I can fight my own battles.''

"Sleeping with that Heart, too?'' Cole asked Lance.

Sonja flinched as if she'd been hit.

Lance advanced on Cole. "You're out of line, Cole.''

Cole raised an eyebrow at Lance, but the younger man stood firm in his challenge. Cole turned his attention on Sonja.

When he'd actually fallen in love with her, he wasn't quite sure. But like a virus, she'd come under or around his defenses when he wasn't looking. And true to virus form, she'd wreaked havoc on his immune system. Mentally older and wiser than he'd been the few short months ago when he met her, Cole knew a hard-line eradication approach was best.

His foolish heart was telling him that he would not have waited this long to finally fall in love with someone who would intentionally or otherwise hurt him. His mind wasn't buying it, though, not in the face of so much contradictory evidence—evidence from her own mouth. His heart told him to trust his gut, but his head said, "No way.''

"I know you have reason to distrust me,'' Sonja said. She reached into the slim attaché case she carried and pulled out a package. Offering it to Cole, she drank in the sight of him, storing up memories for the empty days and nights ahead.

Cole eyed the package as if it were nuclear waste.

"Take it," she said. "It's the least I can do, given my deception. There's a letter, too. It explains everything else you may have wondered about."

When Cole refused to accept the proffered item, Sonja nodded, swallowed, and then handed it to Lance.

"See you around," she told Lance.

With one final look at Cole Heart, the man she'd given her heart to, Sonja turned and walked out of their lives.

# Chapter 19

Cole stood at the front of the small house, waiting for the woman at the door to decide whether to let him in or call the police. More than a week had passed since the Heart shareholders' meeting. He'd done a lot of soul searching in that time. Lance had argued his case, and Sonja's. Cole, listening with half an ear, realized with a sense of pride that this crisis had brought out the best in his nephew. Lance would land on his feet, even if he didn't have a family legacy.

He'd mended fences with Uncle Jimmy and had a lot of questions answered. All these years, Cole had operated under the assumption that Heart Federated was a retail company. Jimmy's take made it sound more like a front agency for a thriving trade in adultery, back stabbing, and shady deals.

"Go do your own thing, boy," Jimmy said. "Be like my daddy and make something happen in this world."

Jimmy encouraged Cole to strike out on his own, to

take his know-how and love for the retail industry and build himself his ideal company. Cole had already decided to do just that. And his uncle wasn't the only person who'd made that suggestion .

Cole smiled and watched suspicion cross the woman's face through the screen.

"What's so funny?"

"Nothing, Mrs. Pride. I just want to talk to you."

She unlatched the door. "The only reason I'm letting you in is what you said in the newspaper."

Cole raised an eyebrow as he stepped into the house. "What's that?"

She paused. "If you don't know what you said, maybe you were lying."

In the last few days, Cole had talked to more journalists than he could count. Heart was one of the last small, family-operated chains. Its dissolution made news. At first Cole was angry, even belligerent, in interviews. Then he thought about Sonja. He thought about the future. He thought about making his own mark, one that didn't have a history tainted with sex scandals, payoffs, and illegitimate children mixed into the business environment.

Cole had no idea what Edith Pride was talking about, but he hadn't come there to get distracted. He came for answers.

"I've never lied," he answered her. "I've come today because I'd like you to know some things. And, if possible, I'd like to find out something from you."

In the long days since the board's vote, Cole had learned to listen to both his heart and his head. They happened to be in accord right now. Confident and secure, he stood before Sonja's mother.

"Mrs. Pride, I love your daughter. I didn't plan on

that happening. The last thing I needed in my life was the complication of a relationship. But that's exactly where I found myself.''

''I personally don't see what she sees in you.''

Cole bit back a smile at the revelation in her words.

''I have to ask you something very personal. You may think it's none of my business, but I have to know. I can't get a straight answer out of Sonja, or any of my relatives.''

''What?''

There was no way to sugar coat the question. ''Was my father, Coleman Heart II,'' he said, adding so there could be no misunderstanding, ''was he Sonja's father?''

Edith's eyes widened. Then she slapped him, hard.

Cole flinched, but he didn't falter.

''How dare you! You Hearts have a lot of nerve, you know.''

Edith raised a hand to hit him again, but Cole intercepted the move and gently held her away.

''Mrs. Pride, I'm in love with Sonja. I want to marry her. Surely you can see the difficulty in that if she's my sister.''

Edith blanched. ''She's agreed to marry you?''

Cole sighed and released her hand. ''Right now, she isn't even talking to me.''

''Good. I raised my baby to be strong, to raise hell.''

Cole could definitely see where Sonja got her backbone.

''Mrs. Pride, you haven't answered my question,'' he said patiently.

She glared at him for a long time. ''You said you're in love with her?''

Cole nodded.

''Why?''

"Why?" he asked back.

Edith put her hands on her hips, and Cole recognized the gesture as one of Sonja's confrontational postures.

"It's not a hard question, Mr. Heart."

Cole smiled. "No, it's not. But the answer is."

"Why don't you give it your best shot?"

Cole looked over Edith's head toward the new voice, one he knew well. Sonja stood in a doorway.

She wore a low, scoop-necked top and a pair of snug-fitting jeans. Keds graced her feet. Cole loved the sight of her. He'd missed her. Did she really love him?

As Lance had pointed out again and again, if Sonja had wanted to see him broken why did she vote with him? If Sonja didn't love him, why did she look so devastated?

Cole's first answer—that the guilt was killing her—didn't add up, particularly after he'd read her letter and her proposal. Like a judge recounting a war criminal's list of atrocities, she detailed every slight she'd ever taken from his family, every wounding of her spirit and her mother's will. In the missive, she explained her plan to sabotage his company, as well as why and how she'd changed her mind. She loved him.

"Women do strange things in the name of love," she wrote. "Since there's no chance for us, enclosed you'll find a second chance for you. No matter what the outcome of the meeting, you were going to get this."

Sonja's package contained an airtight, dynamic business plan that incorporated all the best things he'd ever wanted to see in a business. She'd really been listening as they'd talked hopes and dreams.

Edith glanced at the two, who didn't seem inclined to talk in front of her. "I guess that's my cue to leave."

"No," Cole and Sonja said at the same time.

"I'd like you to hear what I have to say to your daughter, Mrs. Pride. I have no secrets."

Edith looked at Sonja, who nodded. "Okay, Heart. You were saying?"

"Mom, we can sit down for this."

"Well, I guess so." Edith's reluctance to have a Heart in her house came through loud and clear, but one look at her daughter—at the hope and love pouring from her eyes—changed Edith's mind. She'd never seen Sonja like this. Not even when she had her first boyfriend. Maybe Fate knew what it was doing.

Edith led them to the sofa and a chair. The two women sat on the sofa. Cole stood before them.

"Sonja, thank you for all of your support. I know I didn't act very appreciatively the last time I saw you. I am. It's been a difficult time for me. Coping with all of this has been, well, frankly it's been hell." He shrugged. "But the one thing that's given me perspective is you."

Sonja glanced down at her hands.

"I'm sorry about the things I said. There's no excuse for that."

Cole turned to Edith. "In my heart, I know there's no way Sonja could be my sister. I think somehow, some way, I'd know that. But for my own peace of mind, I need your confirmation."

Edith nodded, then pushed herself up from the sofa. "I'll be right back. I need to get a couple of things."

When she left the room, Cole and Sonja stared at each other until the silence became uncomfortable. Embarrassed, she glanced away. Cole cleared his throat.

"I'm sorry about all the things my family did to you," he said. Cole moved toward her and sat on the edge of the chair nearest her. "I'm sorry for everything. From the false shoplifting charge to the scholarship that went to one of my cousins when you deserved it most, I'm sorry.''

"You had nothing to do with it," she said. "It's taken me a while, but I've managed to get over and get beyond all that petty stuff. Holding onto the anger for so many years clouded my judgment.''

"You're wrong, Sonja. I could have made a difference at least on one occasion.''

"What?''

He took her hand in his. "It's always bothered me that I never found out what happened to a little girl who got splashed by my mother's car.''

Sonja's eyes widened, and she yanked her hand from his. "You were one of those kids in the backseat?''

"No," Edith said as she joined them. "My guess is he was the young man who offered us cab fare home that day.''

Cole looked over his shoulder and nodded. He rose as Mrs. Pride joined them. This time, though, she was grinning.

Sonja blushed and helplessly looked at her mom. "Don't say it, Mom, please.''

Edith chuckled. "Uh uh, baby. This is too good. If this is going where I think it's going, he needs to know.''

Curious, Cole looked at them. "Know what?''

Edith settled on the sofa near Sonja. "Are you going to tell him, or am I?''

Sonja covered her face and groaned.

Her mother chuckled. "Guess it's me, then.''

Cole found himself smiling even though he didn't know what was so amusing. He'd never seen this side of Sonja.

"For a long time, Sonja here had a crush on and fantasized about the handsome young businessman who had come to her rescue."

"Mom, please."

But Edith relished the telling. "It's what made everything seem like it was destined to happen. You were the topic of many a refrigerator coloring picture," she told Cole. "You fixed dresses and saved Sonja from bully girls. You even slew a few dragons. I think my favorite one is when you carried Princess Sonja off to your magical kingdom."

Sonja wanted to die of embarrassment. "You didn't have to include examples, Mom."

Enchanted, Cole sat there with a silly grin on his face. "You had a crush on me?"

Sonja's cheeks flamed, and she couldn't meet his gaze.

Cole leaned forward and kissed her on the cheek. "I think that's sweet. It also explains a lot of things," he said, just soft enough for Sonja to hear.

He leaned forward to kiss her. Edith cleared her throat, loudly.

They sprang apart like high school kids caught necking on the sofa.

"Mrs. Pride, I do want to kiss your daughter. Is it legal?"

She nodded. From a velvet-lined box she pulled out a piece of paper, a photograph, and a set of dog tags.

"Sonja's father died in the Vietnam conflict. I was six months pregnant when I got the news he'd been killed in action. His name is on The Wall." She handed Cole the birth certificate and the dog tags.

"I'm sorry,' " Cole said.

"Don't be," Edith said. "He died valiantly."

"If you take a look at that photo and others," Sonja said, "you'll see how much I favor him. I'm not your half-sister, Cole. I don't understand why you'd think we're related."

Edith handed him the photo, Cole glanced at it and then looked between mother and daughter.

"I think you know why, Mrs. Pride. You had to sue my father to stop his harassment. You weren't the only one."

Edith nudged Sonja. "Told you so."

"The possibility was there," Cole told Sonja. "I have one half-sister I know, and apparently some others that I don't. My mother sure believed you were one of them." He nodded toward Edith, "Your mother's case fit the profile and my father's M O."

"I'm not your sister, Cole. I never would have had . . ." she paused, and glanced at her mother.

Edith's gaze dipped to her daughter's stomach. "That your way of telling me I might be a grandma?"

Sonja and Cole stared at each other, each remembering their conversation after a passionate night of unprotected sex.

If Sonja blushed one more time she was going to scream. "Uh," she began.

Edith held up her hand. "I don't want to know."

Cole breathed a sigh of relief. He realized he'd love to see Sonja's belly grow big with his baby. But they had some things to talk about before approaching that. He'd seen the father's name on the birth certificate, and heard what he needed to hear. He had his proof. His gut hadn't let him down.

Now he had to be about the most important business of the day.

"I love you, Sonja Pride. I'm a man without a job and no prospects lined up at the moment, but I have some things going for me."

Crossing her arms, she smiled and leaned back into the sofa. "Like what?"

Cole's own smile grew from tentative to confident. "I had the good sense to fall for you."

She shook her head. "Hmm. Dubious at best. I was out to get you, and you didn't know."

So busy staring at each other, they never noticed when Edith slipped away to give them privacy.

"That's because I was blinded by that red dress with the back out."

Sonja smiled, but then her expression grew somber. "Cole, you weren't the only one at fault."

"You've already apologized in your letter," he said.

"I just want you to know I don't think I would have been able to go through with the plan, even if all systems were perfect. I wouldn't have wanted to."

He switched seats and joined her on the sofa. "I have a suggestion. Let's start over," he said. "I'm going to have to do that, anyway. I love the proposal you put together."

"I've been thinking about it practically since that first night. You were so arrogant, so self-assured. I began thinking about what you might do if you were stripped of all you knew and loved, and had to start over. No silver spoon or golden parachute to cushion the fall."

"It looks like I'll be doing just that. Would you join me? You could be executive vice-president or something."

Sonja shook her head. "Vice president. I don't think so. I'm quite happy being the one in charge. I'm already president of my own company. Besides, I'm knee deep in personnel and staffing problems. This is not the time for me to get distracted with a new business project."

"Anything I can do to help?"

Sonja shook her head. "Everything's under control. I had a senior vice president who left. He thought he was taking half my work force with him. But just three others left, a supervisor and his secretary included." Sonja smiled. "I felt like the mistress of the manor in a medieval novel."

"Why?"

"A lot of people looked at us like a unit, brains and brawn, so to speak. When he left, I guess they felt a need to come swear fealty."

Cole looked at her. "You're kidding?"

Sonja shook her head. "One by one, my managers and supervisors came into my office to declare their loyalty. I almost cried in front of them all at our last large group staff meeting."

"It takes a special person to garner that sort of support."

She shrugged. "I provide a comfortable workplace and jobs that offer both a challenge and to some extent a sense of autonomy. Everyone's opinion is valued, even though I have the last say. By the way, you'll probably hear from him or the company he works for now."

"Whoever it is I won't do business with him."

"Brian Jackson. He's the one who left."

"Ouch. He seemed pretty sharp."

"He is," Sonja said. "We wish him well."

Cole looked at her. "There's more to this story."

"No, not really. Life goes on."

"Well, that leaves just one other type of business for us to discuss," Cole said.

"What business?"

"A merger. A partnership, if you will."

"What kind of partnership? From my view, there are lots of other options and scenarios available to us."

"All destined to failure," Cole said, "all of them except this one."

The kiss, unlike all their others, was a thing of slow passion built over a hot fire. His invitation, a passionate challenge Sonja found difficult to resist, urged her on. She had no desire to resist, particularly when he used that slow hand of his.

She'd fallen for a hard case who would continue to be a demanding handful. Sonja knew they would argue as passionately as they did other things. A delightful shiver of wanting raced through her.

Cole moved from her mouth to her neck, nibbling, tasting, staking his territory. Then he paused, stared into her brown eyes, and kissed her.

"You bring color to my black and white world. Will you let me continue to slay dragons on your behalf? I won't let anyone ruin your Easter dresses, and I'll build you that magical castle if you want it."

Sonja bit her lower lip. Cole took advantage of the sweet invitation and kissed her again.

"What are you asking me, Cole?"

"This is a proposal. I'm proposing a merger."

She nodded. "That's what I thought. I think I forgot to tell you something, Cole."

"Mmm. What's that?" he murmured.

Sonja knew what her heart wanted. And she knew she'd found it in Cole. "I love you."

"Well, it's about time you came to your senses."

She grabbed a throw pillow and bopped him on the head.

"Oh, you want to play rough? I'm game."

Cole maneuvered himself and Sonja so she lay stretched out under him. Starting at the tender edge of her breast, his hand began a slow, stroking descent down her body. Sonja moaned and arched into him.

"Who's the boss?" he asked.

"I am."

Cole's chuckle made her smile. "I think you're right about that. You forever hold the key to my heart."

## ABOUT THE AUTHOR

Felicia Mason is an award-winning journalist and author. Her novels include *Rhapsody, Seduction, For the Love of You,* and *Body and Soul.* In 1997, *For the Love of You* was named one of *Glamour* magazine readers' all-time "Favorite Love Stories."

Mason is a two-time winner of the Best-Selling Multi-cultural Title Award from Waldenbooks. Her work has also received a Reviewer's Choice Award from *Romantic Times,* and the Best Contemporary Ethnic Novel Award from *Affaire de Coeur.*

She lives in Virginia, where she's busy working on her next book.

## ABOUT THE AUTHOR

# COMING IN JANUARY ...

**BEYOND DESIRE**       (0-7860-0607-2, $4.99/$6.50)
by Gwynne Forster
Amanda Ross is pregnant and single. Certainly not a role model for junior high school students, the board of education may deny her promotion to principal if they learn the truth. What she needs is a husband and music engineer Marcus Hickson agrees to it. His daughter needs surgery and Amanda will pay the huge medical bill. But love creeps in and soon theirs is an affair of the heart.

**LOVE SO TRUE**       (0-7860-0608-0, $4.99/$6.50)
by Loure Bussey
Janelle Sims defied her attraction to wealthy businessman Aaron Deverreau because he reminded Janelle of her womanizing father. Yet he is the perfect person to back her new fashion boutique and she seeks him out. Now they are partners, friends ... and lovers. But a cunning woman's lies separate them and Janelle must go to him to confirm their love.

**ALL THAT GLITTERS**       (0-7860-0609-9, $4.99/$6.50)
by Viveca Carlysle
After her sister's death, Leigh Barrington inherited a huge share of Cassiopeia Salons, a chain of exclusive beauty parlors. The business was Leigh's idea in the first place and now she wants to run it her way. To retain control, Leigh marries board member Caesar Montgomery, who is instantly smitten with her. When she may be the next target of her sister's killer, Leigh learns to trust in Caesar's love.

**AT LONG LAST LOVE**       (0-7860-0610-2, $4.99/$6.50)
by Bettye Griffin
Owner of restaurant chain Soul Food To Go, Kendall Lucas has finally found love with her new neighbor, Spencer Barnes. Until she discovers he owns the new restaurant that is threatening her business. They compromise, but Spencer learns Kendall has launched a secret advertising campaign. Embittered by her own lies, Kendall loses hope in their love. But she underestimates Spencer's devotion and his vow to make her his partner for life.

*Available wherever paperbacks are sold, or order direct from the Publisher. Send cover price plus 50¢ per copy for mailing and handling to Kensington Publishing Corp., Consumer Orders, or call (toll free) 888-345-BOOK, to place your order using Mastercard or Visa. Residents of New York and Tennessee must include sales tax. DO NOT SEND CASH.*